SHANNON'S REBIRTH

A gripping, action-packed thriller

PAUL BENNETT

Nick Shannon Thriller Book 8

JOFFE BOOKS

Joffe Books, London
www.joffebooks.com

First published in Great Britain in 2023

Cover art by Nick Castle

ISBN: 978-1-83526-022-7

'The biggest obstacle to good advertising is the client . . .'

Murder must advertise,
Dorothy L Sayers

'. . . especially when he dies on you.'

Nick Shannon

A homage to the Golden Age of crime.

CHAPTER ONE

The yellow Hi-Viz jacket was easy to obtain: there had been one that came with the car for emergency use at night. The hard hat and fire extinguisher were from a common-or-garden builders' merchant. The single security guide looked up from his monitors as I pounded on the glass door of the headquarters of Zeus. He got up from his seat, put his uniform cap on and walked slowly towards me. It was a good job it wasn't a real emergency. When he opened up the door, I yelled at him.

'Reports of a fire on the tenth floor. I've been sent to assess the situation before the fire engine comes. Any people in the offices?'

'Only Sir Gerald Campion, working late for the first time for a long while,' he said.

'Ring him and tell him to stay put before I give him instructions. No one is to enter the building. I'll take the stairs to the tenth floor. The lift is now out of bounds. Keep calm and watchful.'

Duly, I went to the lift and pressed the button. The door slid back and I entered. It seemed to take an age before it got to the ninth floor, my claustrophobia not helping. Every moment lost meant that the guard had more time to think about the unusual situation and question my actions.

I walked to the office that I sought, went through the door and sat down at the desk. I took off the helmet, set it on the desk and placed the extinguisher on the floor. I turned the laptop off and then immediately on, tapping two buttons on the keyboard at the same time. The screen went blank, then turned black with white letters. I was into the realm above the program that existed to let everybody have access to the cloud running all their systems. I inputted a username and crossed my fingers that I had a lazy programmer. I was recognised. Now for the password. Lazy again. I was in.

I called up the program for the finances. Entered the one word — *withdraw*. Plenty in the bank. I tapped in the sum I wanted and waited for the transaction to be verified. Bingo. All done. I sat back in the chair and waited. Not for long.

The door opened and Sir Gerald Campion entered. He was dressed in a handmade suit which coped admirably to mask the bulk from sixty years of his too many Yorkshire puddings and roast beef. It was fitting, too — if you pardon the pun — for the boss of an empire ranging from publishing in traditional formats (magazines, newspapers and periodicals), through broadcasting online and satellite services to gambling in all its forms. Soon, he would rival Sky. That was the goal.

'Well, my boy,' he said. 'Did you do it?'

He called me "my boy" not only for the age difference, but also as he saw me as the son he had never had, and I saw him in return as a father figure. We — Shannon Investigations, fraud detectives — had worked for him uncovering frauds in his gambling division, and he was ever grateful. I now spent two days a month as a non-executive director of Zeus, the parent company. Tonight's mission was about convincing any dissenters that their security needed a lot of work to eliminate any holes which were vulnerable to fraud.

'Too easy,' I said. 'Canning — my computer man, who is in charge of keeping the system at Mid Anglia police force working as it should — gave me all the instructions I needed. It worked like a dream.'

'How did you do it?' he said. 'Although I suppose that is irrelevant. It's the money that counts, isn't it?'

'I'll come to the money in a moment. First, it's how I did it,' I said. 'Getting past the security guard wasn't a problem. Don't be too harsh on him; these were areas he had never dealt with before, and he had to make a snap decision. Moving on to the weakness in the system: When systems are designed, the programmer often puts in a back door. It is the easiest way to run everything. It enables the operator to update the system and install patches — usually eliminating spam or spyware. There are a couple of versions for entry. The most common one is username *sysop* — short for systems operator — and password *sysop*. Using the same username and password means that the operator doesn't have to note down and remember multiple details for all the programs of which he or she is in charge. This programmer took the easiest route and used *sysop*. It meant I had absolute control, and I used it wisely.'

I took a one-pound coin from my pocket and placed it on the desk in front of Campion. 'That's what I owe you.'

'You took a pound?' he said.

'As you said, the amount doesn't matter. It's the security of the system that counts.'

'What do we need to do?' he asked.

'I have no idea. Way beyond me, but my man Canning will fix it for you. He'll work on it alongside his other duties, probably evenings. Reward him handsomely and relax.'

'Arrange it, please,' he said. 'That brings me on to your next task. I had lunch today with the chairman of our advertising agency, Pym's. Like me, he's getting on a bit. Unlike me, he's looking to retire soon. He's going to have a private placement of some of his shares, current employees and outside investors looking for a sound bet — business dragons, white knights and the like. The last audit didn't throw up anything, but he'd like you to check it out and give your seal of approval. See that there aren't any skeletons in the closet. That would reassure any potential investors. He would have been happy to pay your usual fees, but I pushed him up a bit — five thousand pounds a day, plus expenses, plus ten per cent of any fraud found. Do say that you'd do it, if only as a favour to me.'

I nodded.

And that was my first mistake.

CHAPTER TWO

How does the song go? 'When you've got nothing, you've got nothing to lose'. We had everything: a wonderful converted five-storey wharf with fabulous views over the Thames as our home and office; good, loyal friends and workmates; a business that we had expanded because of the publicity after I had killed the Home Secretary — but that's another story. When you've got everything, you've got everything to lose. We were vulnerable. And that is dangerous.

On the ground floor of the wharf, we had an office for me with space for visits from clients, two smaller offices for admin, and an informal sitting area looking over the river with an essential proper coffee machine. The floor above that was for all of us — I'll fill you in on that in a moment — for just relaxing or eating meals together — every storey had its own kitchen.

The floor above that was for Norman — ex-embezzler and cellmate in Chelmsford, who bankrolled us when Shannon Investigations, fraud detectives, was just starting out — and his partner Morag. She was recruited from her job as PA to the Chief Constable of Mid Anglia Police Force after one of our jobs there caused a reorganisation — and the death of the Home Secretary. Did I mention that?

The next storey was occupied by Anji, aged twenty-three, graduate from Exeter in Economics and former pole dancer. Anji was as feisty as they come, and gave us lessons from the present and not the past. She kept us grounded. And was beautiful, too.

The top floor was for me and my partner — fiancée now, marriage to come — Cherry Walker. We'd had a love-hate relationship for many years until my wife passed away. All hate departed, and the space left was filled with love. Cherry was the most beautiful woman I have ever seen. Her natural skin colour was like coffee cream, a throwback to her Iranian roots. She had cheek bones that most women would die for. Her eyes were black and mesmerising — you could lose yourself in them. Her credentials were that she was ex-Fraud Squad, and she had contacts there who would track car registrations, police files and so on, as favours repaying good deeds from the past. Not quite according to the rule book, but who could resist when Cherry called?

There were three people on the payroll who didn't live in — Arthur, Valentine and Beryl. Arthur was my cellmate in Brixton, who taught me how to survive in prison. Not always successfully, but without Arthur, I would not be the same person as I am today. He was an ex-wrestler under the name of Arthur 'Dangerous' Duggan. He was six foot five and looked like a bear, which was descriptive, except he was like a Teddy bear when not threatened.

Beryl was recruited from our job at a law firm where her boss was poisoned — that's the kind of people we were. Dead clients and waifs and strays. Beryl was Morag's assistant.

Our last, and most recent, recruit was Valentine. Twenty-two and lower second from Warwick in Sociology, so not the best CV in the jobs market. More relevant to his past career, however, was that he was the son of the CEO of Zeus, David Shapiro. We rescued him from a life of tedium into our world of adventure, corpses included. And he was a babe magnet.

As I said — we have everything. Now read on.

* * *

We sat on the ground floor in the area overlooking the river sipping drinks, catching up and constructing a game plan. Norman and Morag on one of the three Chesterfields arranged in an open square so as not to obscure the view; Cherry and Beryl sat on another and Valentine on the third. Anji sat on the floor in a yoga position between Valentine's legs.

'What's the latest on the Silvers' job?' I asked Cherry. Silvers was an investment bank where they needed another eye over their money-laundering protocol. 'How long before we can get that out of the way?'

'End of the week,' she replied. 'Valentine and I are going to draft the outline of the report tomorrow. Do you need us?'

'We're going to be doing this as a favour to Sir Gerald, as well as for Pym's. I'd like to wrap it up as soon as possible. As we know, he's not the most patient man.'

'But not a bad person for that,' said Cherry. 'He's more of a friend than a client.' She checked her watch — a Cartier Santos with the gold screws to match mine, both thank-you presents from Sir Gerald after our work on Zeus' gambling divisions. 'Are we going to double up on this job?'

'I think so,' I said. 'You and Valentine as a team, and Anji and I together, if that's OK with you all.'

Anji and Valentine nodded.

'Anything else in the diary?' I asked Morag.

'A couple of briefing meetings set for next week, but this week clear.'

'So where do we start?' said Norman. 'You can put me down for research. Not that I know anything about advertising.'

'That goes for all of us,' I said. 'But we're quick learners.'

'So it's down to Pym's for you tomorrow, then?' said Cherry.

'Not immediately,' I said.

'So where do we start?' asked Anji.

'We start at the horse's mouth.'

CHAPTER THREE

Anji and I drove to Zeus headquarters and encountered the first hurdle of the day. The car park was closed for resurfacing. It said so in the hastily drawn A4 notice — hastily drawn because the writer couldn't spell *resurfacing*, the *u* replaced by another *e*. We headed back to the roads surrounding the site and found spaces hard to come by. We got out and prepared for a walk of about a mile. Anji was in professional mode — false glasses, black skirt to the knee, white blouse and flat pumps rather than heels. No problem for the walk.

'Nice car, mister,' came the voice of a young boy as we got out. 'Wouldn't want to see its tyres cut or a key run along the side. I'll mind it for you.'

He was around thirteen or fourteen, I guessed, wearing grey baggy pants and a black hoody, which was down. He had brown hair and eyes and was as thin as a razor blade.

'And how much will this protection cost?' I said.

'Twenty quid, and cheap at the price. Lots of rough types around. Good job you met me. I don't know what would have happened otherwise.'

I liked his bare-faced cheek. I took a ten-pound note and gave it to the lad. 'Half now and the other half if you're still here when we come back.'

'Deal,' he said.

'What's your name, kid?'

'Why do you want to know?'

'I like to know who I'm doing business with.'

'You can call me Buzz like everyone else does — won't get you any more protection, though. And I ain't a kid. I can look after myself.'

'Why aren't you in school?' I said.

'School doesn't care,' he said. 'What's the use anyway? Won't find me a job. I'll scratch a living somewhere.'

'I'll give you an extra ten pounds if you take me to where you hang out.'

'What are you?' he said. 'Some kind of paedo?'

'I'm not a paedo,' I said.

'I can vouch for that,' said Anji. 'Believe me, he just likes lost causes.'

* * *

Andrew Hamilton was Group Marketing Director of Zeus — all three divisions reported to him. I wanted to get his views on the performance of Pym's, so as to see what clients wanted from their advertising agency and whether Pym's met their needs: the more Pym's fell short, the lower the value of the shares. I had met Andy once before at my first board meeting and warmed to him. It was a good place to start.

He rose from his seat to shake my hand and gestured for us to sit down opposite. There was an insulated flask of coffee on his desk with milk and sugar, and he poured me a cup. He was tall and toned from his daily ritual of a five-mile morning run. I had been able to talk socially with him at the end of the board meeting, so didn't have to start from square one. I had learnt of his wife and two young boys and how important they all were to him — a photo of the four of them on his desk substantiated it.

His appearance could only be described — by those who still use that word — as dapper. He was wearing a light grey suit with a pink handkerchief folded in the top pocket. His shirt matched the handkerchief and the sleeves peeked out from the jacket, showing silver cuff links with the design of an elephant — is 'never forget' what they were intended to show? His tie was plain blue and done in a classic double-Windsor knot. His brown hair showed the first flecks of grey at the temples and his green eyes smiled at me.

'So you cracked the system, Sir Gerald tells me,' he said. 'Thinks of you as some kind of wunderkind. Hard to deny.'

'I had a lot of help,' I said. 'You get to make a lot of useful friends in my business, not all of them legal. I was just following a recipe, like making a cake.'

'With no soggy bottoms.'

'With no soggy bottoms,' I said. 'Like much of life, it's down to perfect timing.'

'What can I do for you?' he said. 'Sir Gerald said it was something to do with Pym's. I'm not sure I can help you much — I leave the mechanics to the three marketing directors below me.'

'How long has Pym's been your agency?'

'Since I joined Zeus some five years ago. New broom and all that. Happens all the time. Existing agencies start to take you for granted. Pym's had a strong creative department and an impressive showreel. The presentation was slick, and they filled me with confidence.'

'Since then?' I asked. 'Any regrets?'

'They need watching, keeping on their toes, so I'm told. Their admin and accounts can be a bit sloppy — run-of-the-mill procedures that should be second nature.'

'At the board meeting, you showed me what you called a dashboard. A lot of figures boiled down to a few traffic lights — brand awareness, advertising awareness and effectiveness, brand image on a number of constituent parts, customer satisfaction and so on. Is that how you judge them? Get as many green lights as you can?'

'Afraid to say so,' Andy said. 'Not much time at a board meeting to go deeper, as you know. If there's anything going wrong, we then discuss it.'

'So what are you looking for from Pym's?' I asked. Leave the vital question to last, when the respondent relaxes and thinks it's all over bar the shouting.

'At the heart of the budget, spending a great deal with our satellite services has to be a factor. They're strong on media planning and buying. We're not unhappy with the overall campaign.'

'Damned by faint praise,' I said.

'You're really going to shake things up, aren't you?' he said.

'Well, someone's got to.'

'And it might as well be you.'

'Exactly.'

* * *

Buzz was waiting for us, sitting on the bonnet of the Beamer, smoking a thin roll-up and looking cool. He watched mesmerised as Anji took the clips from her hair and shook her head to let her blonde hair fall to her shoulders. 'Wow,' he said. 'Some chick.'

He was going to be putty in our hands.

'Let's start walking,' I said. 'Lead the way.'

He walked with a swagger like you would see from a hero in a western movie, rocking side by side, his shoulders going up and down in time with his steps. From time to time he looked back at Anji, as if to check she was real and not part of some teenage imagination.

We arrived at a piece of wasteland which had once had a bungalow on it. It was now a complete burnt-out ruin. A group of about eight young boys were sat around on a slab of concrete that had served as the foundations of the house. They were smoking — God knows where they got the money from. But what else did they have to do? These were kids that had no future. How can we let that happen?

'Do you have a leader?' I asked.

'That would be me,' answered a tall, well-built lad. I reckoned how he had been chosen — strongest boy — but not necessarily the brightest.

'Your name?' I said.

'What's that to do with you?'

'Because I'm going to save you from a life of boredom. So, let's start again. What's your name?'

'I'm Chip. That's what everyone calls me.'

Chip off the old block, or chip on his shoulder? Big difference.

'So what do you guys do all day?' I asked.

'Hang around, you know, chew the fat,' Chip said.

There must be a hell of a lot of fat to chew to do it every day, all of the time.

'So what's wrong with school?' I said.

He laughed. 'They class us as Special Needs. Separate us from the rest of the school. Put us down at every opportunity. Nothing special about it. A lot of hate, though.'

'What do you live on?' I asked.

'Small money from our parents. Earn a bit on top of that.'

'Shoplifting?'

'There might be some of that,' said Chip. 'Most of the shops know us. Turn a blind eye.'

'Any opposition? Rival gangs?' I said.

'The Sharks are the worst. Think they control the territory and can do what they like.'

'Any of you carry weapons? Show them to me.'

Frightening. Half the boys drew out an array of knives.

'And how many of you want to spend the rest of your life in prison?'

Rhetorical question.

'Buzz, take me on a tour of your patch. The rest of you, same place, same time tomorrow.' No one needed to check with a diary.

We walked for a while, passing blocks of flats with depressive frontages hiding more depression inside. There was a feeling that everybody here had given up hope. At the bottom of one block, there were a few shops: a newsagent/tobacconist/sweets and other impulse purchases, a general store with racks of exotic vegetables outside; launderette; a shop selling second-hand furniture; a pawnshop probably doing more trade than all the other shops put together. There was a hairdressers, now empty and boarded-up. A growing trend, I suspected. Soon there would be no life worth living here.

'This is it,' Buzz said. 'This marks the boundary with the Sharks. We both claim it. That's why we fight.'

'Over this?' I said, incredulous. 'A few grotty rundown shops? This is what's worth carrying knives for?'

'Give 'em an inch and they'll take a mile,' Buzz said. 'I suppose you could call it a matter of principle.'

Never too young to have principles, I thought, but this was misguided, and could only lead to trouble, prison-style.

As we walked back, the chill of the evening had begun. Maybe they huddled together for warmth as well as protection.

'Same time, same place tomorrow,' I said to the gang. 'Don't forget. I may have a surprise for you.'

'What's the surprise going to be?' Anji said, when we were away.

'I'm going to unleash Arthur on them.'

CHAPTER FOUR

The office of Vernon Pym's was on the top floor of a building in the heart of Soho, squeezed between a film production company and a Chinese restaurant, of which there were many in what is called Chinatown. The chances of parking there were non-existent, so Anji and I drove the Beamer back home and took the Docklands Light Railway from Island Gardens. Mostly overground, it was interesting to see the way the east of London had developed over the years since Docklands had been formed and become a hot area for property.

It was lunchtime by the time of our arrival, so we popped into the next-door restaurant and had a light selection of dim sum. Just the ticket. Anji asked me where we would start.

'At the top of the pyramid,' I said. 'Vernon Pym. Unless we get his full cooperation — and there's no reason not to — then nobody will talk. After him, the finance director — get approval and passwords for entry to the system. Then we fit in who we can. Tomorrow, interview other key members of the agency and slog through the accounts, turning over stones and see what lies beneath.'

'And what is my role?' she asked.

'You'll be my assistant — we might as well start with the truth before resorting to misdirection. Take notes of what's said and the body language that goes with it — most people find it hard to lie convincingly, but maybe things are different in advertising, par for the course. See if I make Pym sweat at any time. Tomorrow will be a fact-finding mission of the main players, as well as the accounts department.'

'Am I dressed right?' she asked. 'You know the Little-Miss-Librarian look? The false glasses and such.'

'Hard to tell. I assume the top people will be in suits and the ones that do the work will be fashionably casual, but that might just be prejudice or watching too much *Mad Men*. We'll play it by ear now, and make any changes tomorrow to blend in.'

And so, strategy sorted, we entered the offices through a glass door with the name *Pym's* engraved in italic script. Note the apostrophe. Belonging to Pym.

You can tell a lot about a company by its reception area. It is the first place that a visitor sees. It is — or should be — the summation of the company ethos. It is the pulsing heart of the company. *Slick* was my first impression. The reception area was minimalistic. No clutter anywhere. Lots of glass and chrome sparkling. Director chairs in chrome with black leather backs. A desk with a glass top and a modesty panel of black, at which a perfectly dressed woman sat with a warm smile. Two televisions — one showing Zeus News, muted, and the other a showreel of the agency's commercials, not muted. I felt that I was being indoctrinated into a new religion, where only essentials were allowed, and if you didn't have something that needed selling, you should turn round and walk out of the door.

The receptionist made a call on her phone and, while waiting for us to be collected, issued us with lanyards carrying badges marked 'visitor'. In many companies, the badges could carry the pseudonym 'leper', summing up the way they were looked at by staff suspicious of why the visit. We'd see how Pym's did.

A woman aged about fifty appeared, in a classic suit of blue and a white blouse. The skirt length matched her age, slightly below the knees, plus sensible shoes to cope whatever life threw at her. She introduced herself as Ms Brooks, personal assistant to Vernon Pym. She shook our hands, and we were led to an antiquated lift serving the five storeys of the building. It was one of those lifts that was twice-gated, one inside the lift and another on each floor, and couldn't operate unless both gates were securely closed. Inside, there was a lift attendant in a smart black suit who looked like an ex-marine and had muscles big enough to cope with the gates. He ushered us inside and set about the gates. The lift gave me little confidence as it clanked upwards. It would have a finite life, and I didn't want to be in it when it gave its last breath. I vowed to play it safe and use the stairs in future.

Vernon's office was a large rectangular room with a desk and three chairs at one end, and three settees and a coffee table at the other end. On the walls were framed copies of awards that the agency had won. They were mostly a few years old. Every picture tells a story.

His desk was finely polished mahogany and held a set of bottled inks and other stationery, along with a paperweight, atop some clear plastic files. There were no pictures to remind him of family. He got up from his seat — below average height, which caused a momentary frown when he inwardly acknowledged the comparison to my six-three — and shook our hands. Draped over the back of his chair was a tweed jacket with leather protectors on the elbows, the sort that a country squire would wear when processing among his serfs. He had on a white shirt with those elasticated bands that keep the cuffs from being rubbed by his desk. The shortened shirt sleeves showed an expensive watch — Rolex Oyster Perpetual? — on his left arm and a rubber band on the other. Interesting.

He was stick thin and had bald patches of hair on his head that looked like they'd been cut by a barber with his eyes closed. None of that was particularly remarkable. What was, however, was his colour — he was yellow all over, judging from the parts I could see. Skin on his hands yellow, eyes

16

yellow. Either the man had hepatitis, in which case we should hastily retreat, or he was an alcoholic destroying his liver.

He was drinking a cup of coffee when we arrived and asked us if we would like some. I readily agreed, hoping he wouldn't use the telephone to order it from his PA. I was in luck — he got up from his chair and walked to the anteroom where Ms Brooks worked. As soon as he left the room, I bent over his coffee cup and sniffed. Whisky. Sure as day. That settled it. He was drinking himself to death. We were going nowhere.

'Now,' he said, while we were sipping our coffee, 'tell me what you need to know.'

'I only know what Sir Gerald told me, and that was not much. He said you were planning a private placement of shares, and want us to give approval that all is what it seems, financial-wise. Any gaps you can fill in would help us massively.'

'Let's take it from the beginning and see where that takes us,' he said.

Anji raised her pen above her pad. She nodded to me that she was ready.

'It all started,' he continued, 'when my grandfather, a humble printer scraping a living, was asked to publish some Methodist tracts. He did the job well and realised he could make some money by printing some advertisements inside the tracts. And that is where Pym's was born. More ads sold. Bigger tracts sold, and he designed each one perfectly. Now he had creation as well as execution. He grew and prospered, passing the business down the patriarchal line. I am the third generation.'

The first generation makes money, the second consolidates, the third loses it. That's how the saying goes. Would Vernon conform?

'Is there a fourth generation?' I said.

'My son is revolted by the world of advertising. Selling things that people could well do without. Who needs a toothpaste that, allegedly, does six things when a cheaper

17

one would suffice? Does a car really need a bikini-clad bimbo in ridiculous heels to sit on its bonnet? Using the powers of persuasion to manipulate people. To him, advertising is a dirty word. He takes my money, though. His morals seem to allow that. What does this young lady think?'

She looked at me and I nodded.

'I would say he has a point,' Anji said. 'Couldn't the money spent be used for better things?'

'It is the nature of man to compete, to go for the kill,' he said. 'Doing away with advertising wouldn't stop that. But we stray. To get back to the original question, it's time for me to take a back seat. Hungry wolves gather at my door, anxious to have their name on it. That's the goal of many an ad man. And if they don't get their way, they leave, often taking their clients with them. That's no good to anyone. I'll have a private placing of my shares — some will effectively be a management buyout; the rest will be likely taken out by an institutional investor, pension fund and the like.'

'Will you retain any of your shares?' I asked.

'Just enough to secure me the post of non-executive chairman. Give me something to do when I retire. I'll continue to cast my eye over the clients I currently handle, make sure they don't leave.'

'Who are the wolves?' I said.

'For you to grasp that, you need to know the structure.' He took a sip of his whisky-laced cold coffee. 'The main board consists of myself, the creative director, media director and finance and heads of account management and planning. Each client will have a team of an account director — not main board — creative team of copywriter and art director; fancy title for the one who draws the pictures — account planner, media planner and buyer. There will also be others involved in production — the cut-and-paste people, those who turn concepts into fully-finished ads and commercials. The main-board directors will want a slice of the action, and, I suspect, some of the senior team, too. Here's a list of the people you should talk to while you look at the finances.'

He passed across a hand-written sheet of paper. 'I've added a couple of the creative teams — that's the thing that counts in the final analysis. Ms Brooks — Pamela, but known as Brookie — will look after you and arrange interviews. She'll get you an office to work from, and guide you through your process. She's been with me now for fifteen years. She knows more about the place than anyone else. Everyone knows why you're here, so you won't need to explain that.'

'One last thing,' I said. Anji handed me two sheets of paper. 'The contract. Sign both copies and retain one for your records.' I passed them over to Pym. He looked at the contract.

'This bit about ten per cent of any fraud discovered. You won't make much from that. We're watertight.'

'That's what they all say,' I said with a smile.

He signed with a Mont Blanc fountain pen, blew on it to help dry the ink and handed one of the copies to me. I gave it to Anji and stood up to leave. We shook hands — his was trembling — and went to see Brookie. I wondered if part of her duty was to keep the booze cupboard stocked. It seemed to me that he needed another fix.

Brookie led us down a flight of stairs to an office set up as a meeting room with a round table and four chairs. It was bigger than the broom cupboards that were usually assigned to us. It was light and airy and would be a pleasant working environment. The round table had sunk into it power points and sockets for computers to be plugged in. There was a sideboard in the same light veneer as the table, with thermos flasks of what I took to be coffee and tea, all the necessary things like milk and sugar, a plate of custard creams and a set of water bottles, still and sparkling. We were being treated well. We'd see what the reaction was when we started asking questions.

'Did Mr Pym tell you about the fair?' Brookie said.

I shook my head. 'Never came up,' I said.

'Each year, Pym's holds a fair for clients and staff and their families. It's become a tradition that everyone looks forward to. There's a proper funfair run by travellers, with rides and even a ghost train, bouncy castles, plenty of food stalls and a tent for beer and one for tea and cakes. This year's one is on Saturday. It would be an opportunity for you to meet some people outside their offices. I'll send you details. Don't miss it. You'd regret it. It's great fun. Now, who would you like to see and when?'

'Start at the top,' I said. 'Finance director as soon as possible, then I'd like to see the coal face — those who do the actual work. Let's go for whichever creative team is free this afternoon. Tomorrow, we'll start with some of the other directors at hourly intervals. I doubt we'd need them for that long, and we can go through the accounts during the rest of the time. I'll need personnel files, as well.'

'I'll pop back later with a schedule. Let me know if you need anything, more coffee and the like.'

When she was gone, we helped ourselves to coffee and the odd custard cream, three being an odd number, and sat down opposite each other. 'What did you make of Pym?' I asked Anji.

'From your reaction, there was some kind of alcohol in his coffee. Not vodka, as you wouldn't be able to smell that. Whisky or brandy. Brandy is more a drink for the evening, so I'd go for whisky.'

'Correct,' I said. 'The yellow eyes?'

'Liver damage. Too much booze and no desire to stop.'

'The rubber band?'

'Certainly strange. Expensive watch on one wrist — I bet he doesn't know how to operate the bezel and all those buttons, bought for show — and rubber band on the other. Must have some significance, but I have to admit I'm puzzled.'

'It's a sign that he's been to Alcoholics Anonymous. If you get a longing for a drink, you get hold of the band, stretch it and let it go. The sharp pain makes you concentrate on something else and take away the longing for a while.'

'If he's been to AA, then why the whisky in the coffee?'

'He's not beaten it yet. Maybe he's given up, or not reached the low point where you push away the bottle. He's not free of it. Freedom is just another word for nothing left to lose.'

'You're very philosophical today,' Anji said. 'If you don't mind me saying so.'

'We all have our failings,' I said. 'Doesn't do to bring them to the front of the mind. There's a wedding to arrange, and I wonder whether I am good enough for Cherry.'

'At the risk of a new student giving advice to the master, Cherry wouldn't have you any other way. You're a kind man and you love her. That's all you need to know. What you have is not a failing; it's just nerves. There's been plenty of occasions you've faced more dangerous situations than a wedding. Just be yourself.' She paused for thought. 'Hell, this is getting awkward. At any moment, I could put my foot in it. Let's refill our coffees and chase up our appointment to the finance director. Be good to think of something else.'

'Thanks,' I said. 'Good plan. I've gone from doubtful to melancholy — never a good position. Time to get back to the Shannon we all know and love — well, not all. Time to go back to smartarse. The game is on.'

CHAPTER FIVE

Brookie returned after half an hour and presented us with an action-packed schedule for today, Friday, and the start of the following week, and the personnel files we had requested. We climbed the stairs to where the senior players had their offices. Victor O'Hara's was in one corner of the building and had two windows looking over Soho. It was, quite naturally, smaller than Pym's — you can't outdo the boss man. As with many a large organisation, the further you got up the greasy pole, the bigger the office and the more windows you had. In addition to a glass-topped desk and four chairs, there was just one sofa and a small coffee table.

We made our introductions and he motioned us to sit down opposite him across the desk. It was made of a black wood that I reckoned, by the grain, was oak. On the desk was a family photo of O'Hara, wife and two daughters aged around eight or nine, all with blonde hair and sparkling green eyes. By contrast, O'Hara's hair was grey and thinning. Just out of his reach at the moment was a packet of Marlboro and a gold Dunhill lighter. I wondered how many times of day he had to brave the lift to pop out for a sneaky fag. What better reason for giving up smoking?

He was dressed in a black suit and plain white shirt, together with a tie that was decorated with a golden lion, which was so out of keeping that it was almost surely a present from the children. Apart from the tie, he blended in with the desk and chair. The walls matched his shirt. He made a good impression of a chameleon. He spoke quietly with a soft Irish lilt as if apologising for breaking some unwritten rule. He didn't command the stage.

'I have got you two terminals and passwords to access the accounts,' he said. 'I've allowed you full access, just as we do for the auditors. I have fixed you up external access, too, so you can work from anywhere. The last audit was just six months ago, so I shouldn't think it will take you long to verify their figures.'

'I'm more interested in the present than the past,' I said. 'By the way, I like the tie.'

'Birthday present from the twins,' he said.

I realised I would be just showing off in front of Anji if I explained my deductions. 'What are the differences?' I said, 'I should know about how Pym's finances are handled compared with your competitors and business in general.'

'The standard commission we charge is fifteen per cent — that's common practice from way back, no difference from other agencies. Media invoices have to be paid within fourteen days, so clients have to follow suit. On any other services — advertisement productions like making TV commercials or print media — we add 17.65 per cent, which equates to fifteen per cent of the total. Quite easy, when you get the hang of it.'

'And out of that fifteen per cent,' I said, 'how much of that goes into the pocket of Pym's when you've paid all the staff and other expenses?'

'Our net profit is only around four per cent, salaries being the main cost. This is a people business. If we could get salaries down, we'd make about six per cent.'

'And that would be attractive to investors?' I asked.

'Certainly. More than they could get from most investments. Outside investors would probably want a staff cull, too, pushing up our margin.'

'How much, otherwise, are you planning to tweak the figures to get costs down and make that investor-friendly?'

'Only by getting new clients,' he said. 'We're pretty good at housekeeping. Little costs to be cut by buying fewer ballpoints and the like. We run a tight ship.'

Housekeeping. Tight ship. I wondered whether it was a requirement for ad men to speak in metaphors.

'Who would be the staff that would be let go in that cull?' I asked.

'A few admin staff, but the biggest reduction would be in copywriters and art directors. We'd have to get rid of one of our five creative teams, making the remaining four service more clients.'

'I'm told everyone knows what the future plan is,' I said. 'Are there any worries that they're not safe in their jobs?'

'We're pitching it as an opportunity to grow, with the backing of a sizeable investment from internal and external investors,' he said.

Euphemisms as well as metaphors. I was impressed. I was reminded of the old Native American saying: *white man speak with forked tongue.*

'What's your background, Mister O'Hara?' I said.

'I can't see that that is relevant,' he replied.

'You've implied that investors would be buying your staff, who you seem prepared to shed. Staff, especially the creative teams, are the biggest draw for investors — that's the name of the game. If staff were to leave after the placement, the value of the agency would diminish. So, unlike the auditors, I need to understand the staff. That means their backgrounds and how they got here, and how they think and feel today. So, I repeat the question. Tell me about yourself.'

'Irish, but I think you would have realised that from my accent and mode of speech — I don't have the speed of a Northern Irish speaker, so must be Southern Irish — Ireland,

God's own country. Did an accountancy degree at Dublin, a university to rival the best in Great Britain. I'm proud of it. Got a job with a small provincial advertising agency. Got some valuable experience and moved to a bigger one, and then came to England, where the riches were. Ground my way up and this job came up. Been here two years now. I'm paid well and it's a nice working environment, more like a happy family than places I've worked before. What do you make of that?'

'Tip of the iceberg, maybe. Will you be buying shares?' I asked, wondering whether I would get a straight answer.

'If the price is right and I can get a bigger mortgage, then yes. As I've said, it would be a good investment. More than I could get by letting my money languish in some bank account.'

'Are salaries competitive, or more or less than the competition?' I said.

'More, I would say. Pym is weak if an employee comes to him saying they're leaving because they could earn more elsewhere. He gives in and matches that salary, but woe betide it if your face doesn't fit. He'll call your bluff, shake your hand and you're off. No second chances. Result? No wreckers of the Pym's way. No upsetting of the happy family. Only true believers here. Nothing to upset the apple cart.'

I looked across at Anji. Let her have a turn.

'Your children look lovely,' she said. 'Are there decent schools in your area?'

'Nice one, girl,' he said. 'I can see where you're coming from. No, the local schools aren't good. Yes, they're in private education. Yes, I can afford it, and have no reason to rob Pym's.'

She didn't blush. I was interested about how she would follow up next.

'And your new bigger mortgage,' she persisted, brushing his barb aside. Calling her *girl* would not have gone down well either. 'Could you afford that, too?'

'Yes, I can,' he said. 'I have a love of money, true, and a fascination for it, but that's all I get from this job. The satisfaction I get is purely from keeping everything under control. You can carry on digging at me, but you won't find any weaknesses or reasons for me to do anything illegal. I am not an embezzler. And in future, I would be grateful if you would put any questions to my accounts manager.'

I didn't think we would get any more from him. Didn't make any friends, but we'd shaken the tree and seen what fruit had fallen to the ground. Useful? Who knows? What was certain was that we hadn't made a fan in O'Hara. Can't win them all.

'We have the next two people to see,' I said to Anji, when we got back to the privacy of our lavish office. 'And so the hamster wheel goes on. We've got half an hour before then. Time to familiarise ourselves with the way their accounts are managed. A decent cup of coffee would be good, too.'

'How do I always know what is running through your mind?' Anji said.

'Because there are times when I am predictable. When I let my guard down. But, importantly, I'm not always predictable. That would not be good. Predictability is a weakness. It makes you vulnerable. Look and learn, Anji. Look and learn.'

* * *

'Well, if it isn't the illustrious Shannon,' a languid voice, as yet unnamed, said as we entered the room.

There were three people, not two as I had expected, in the room. It was fitted with a long narrow wooden desk, an Anglepoise lamp, a dark green leather sofa and a keyboard and synthesiser in one corner. The one who spoke was sat in a swivelling chair by an open window. There was a rebellious smell of weed in the air. He had blond hair and blue eyes that flashed at me. He was dressed in a pair of light grey trousers, a blue blazer with gold buttons and a pink shirt with a light blue tie. His skin appeared flawless, concealed by a liberal layer of bronzing make-up. His shoes were black suede loafers with a gold buckle. I put his age at twenty-five, although it was hard to guess with the concealing bronzer on his face.

'And who have you brought with you?' he said. 'Your pet librarian?'

'Anji,' I said, 'let your hair loose and shake your head.'

She took the clips out and her long blonde hair fell down past her shoulders.

'Take off the glasses,' I said.

Her beautiful blue eyes glinted in the light from the Anglepoise lamp.

'Roll your skirt up.'

She hitched up her skirt by three inches and rolled it over. Her long slim legs were on full display.

'Undo two buttons of your blouse.'

She undid the buttons so that the curve of her breasts showed.

'What have we here?' he said. 'Anji has had her rebirth, her epiphany. She has experienced her Damascene moment. She is a different woman. A butterfly has emerged from the chrysalis. Oh, how I misjudged you. And have I done the same with you, Shannon? Are you more than you seem? Have you had a rebirth, too?'

'Not yet,' I said, 'but I'm working on it. Why don't we start again?'

'Of course,' he said. 'Killed anyone recently?'

'I'm working on that, too,' I said. 'As we speak.'

'Touché,' he said. 'Oh, what fun we are going to have. Introductions. Tony Lancaster, copywriter, composer of jingles — I shall write one for you — and budding novelist, but all things are possible. To my right is my art director colleague, Ned Cork — good solid name, don't you think? To my left, Matthew Bradley, brand manager at Seeco crisps and snacks. What a cosy triumvirate we are.'

Cork had an A3 layout pad on his lap and was busy doodling. When introduced, all he had done was grunt. From what I could tell with him being seated, he was a classic mesomorph — short, stocky and muscular. He had brown eyes, long hair and a jaw that jutted out. He reminded me of a neanderthal, more suited to a club in his hand than a pencil.

I wondered whether they had to constantly get new carpets because of his knuckles scraping on the floor. He was late twenties and was dressed in denim jeans and a skin-tight white T-shirt that made the most of his muscles. He was the sort of guy you didn't want to meet in a back alley on a dark night. On the wall next to his desk was a collection of framed paintings which, by their crudity, was probably his handiwork. There was no merit in them.

Bradley had on the mandatory blue suit, white shirt and no tie. It was an attempt to appear younger and more fashionable than his middle-aged years, and which didn't work. His dark hair was receding at the temples and beginning to turn grey. As he slouched in the chair, the bulge around his stomach was plain to see. The predominant feature of his face was sticking-out, taxicab, ears. If it was me, I would have gone to a plastic surgeon in my teenage years or grown my hair much longer — rock-style length. He looked at me challengingly, for what reason I did not know. Still, it was early days. The Shannon magic personality had yet to hit him full on.

'May we sit?' I said, annoyed that we were not invited earlier, and by the friction that was, for some reason, filling the air.

'Please do,' said Lancaster, 'Although whatever it is you want will hopefully not take long. After our meeting with friend Bradley here, we have the weekly cut-and-paste bore for our supermarket client. Life is not always peachy.'

The word *peachy* was interesting. I wondered if his novel was private-eye American noir. Hints of Chandler?

'So what can we do for you, dear Shannon?'

'You can start with how you fit in with the food chain that, at the top, is a well-crafted ad.'

'Simple,' Lancaster said. 'I write the words for our clients, and jingles throughout the agency, and Ned does the visuals, but before that is the task of coming up with the ideas. We, Ned and I, are on concept as well as execution.'

'Ably assisted by me as client,' Bradley said.

'In what way?' Anji said, playing dumb blonde to appear less clever than what she was, thus posing no threat to them.

To appear defenceless and come from under their radar. Smart move.

'I make sure they keep on the right track,' Bradley said, with all his attention on Anji's legs. 'Correct me if I am wrong, Tony, but there can be a tendency among creatives to get carried away by an idea, lose sight of the objectives and the brand values that need to be communicated.'

Ned grunted and stared at Anji. If she couldn't warm his heart, what chances did I have?

'Does Matthew know why I am here?' I asked.

'Of course, Matthew knows,' Lancaster said. 'Everyone knows. Everyone is agog to see you. It's not every day you get to meet an ex-convict who's also a killer.'

'I'm not ashamed to carry that label. What I did was honourable, and honour must be observed in a civilised society,' I said. 'Now, what do you think about the idea of a placement of shares? Are you up for buying some?'

'Strangely,' he said, 'I'm tempted, but that is a game too rich for me. I leave all that to the men in suits — no offence, Matthew — and, more importantly, I don't think I could raise that kind of money on a humble copywriter's salary. Maybe when my novel is published, it might be possible.'

'I take it that it will be autographical,' I said. 'Most first novels are. Had a suspenseful childhood, have you, Mister Lancaster? Lots of material to draw upon?'

'Middle-class upbringing. Classics at Cambridge — double first. Rather like you, Shannon, it will be about rebirth. I might come to you for some background material. But maybe you haven't been reborn yet. There's a dark side to you that I could draw upon.'

Time to get on before I lost patience.

'And your background, Ned?' I said, to see if he could do anything except grunt.

'Art college,' he said. And that was it.

'Which leaves only me,' said Bradley. 'Business studies degree at Southampton. Lower second. Joined Seeco as a graduate trainee and been there ever since. How's that for loyalty?'

Loyalty because he couldn't get a higher-paid job elsewhere?

'You asked about the pecking order,' Lancaster said. 'If you haven't found out already, you will soon see that the creatives rule the roost. Without us there would be no ideas, no clients and no agency.'

'Does that also apply to what you called the bore of the weekly supermarket ad?' Anji said, to allow me time to keep my temper under control.

'The deals of the week,' Lancaster said. 'They send the photos and the prices, and we do what we can to write copy to make the dull products more exciting and line it all up on the page nice and neatly. Tedious in the extreme. Have you seen our work on Seeco? "When you Seeco you know it's quality". Pleased with that, eh, Matthew?'

'Catchy little jingle, too,' Matthew said. 'No one can stop humming it. Everyone back at the ranch is pleased, and that's a bonus point for me.'

'Bask in our light, Matthew,' Lancaster said.

Ned tore a sheet from his artist's pad, crossed the room and handed it to Anji. It was a sketch of her when she had dropped her librarian pose. It failed to capture the warmth in her eyes and the depth of beauty in her face. OK, it was done in a few moments, but if I were an artist, I would not have been proud of it. It was an embarrassment and should have gone straight in the bin. It showed bad judgment. Anji took it and smiled, so as not to hurt his feelings, before putting it in her briefcase prior to put it aside for recycling.

Tony got up and went to sit down at the keyboard. He started to play.

'Shannon, oh Shannon.
Don't look him in the eye.
The chances are that if you do,
You're surely going to die.'

The tune was derivative, the words designed to insult. I said nothing.

'Is that all, Shannon?' he said, when he had finished.

'Just one question,' I said.

'Fire away,' Lancaster replied.

'What is the question we should have asked?'

He laughed and shook his head. 'You'll never know, Shannon. You'll never know.'

* * *

We called it a day. There wasn't much to achieve before Monday's meetings, and we could work on the accounts just as well from the office. As we sat in our seats in an empty carriage on the DLR, we reviewed the day. The creatives dominated our thinking.

'Why so aggressive?' Anji asked. 'You couldn't cut the atmosphere with a well-honed sabre.'

'Show of power,' I said. 'Put us in our place. They reckon that they can get away with murder.'

'Like the weed?' she said. 'Not only is smoking banned, but taking drugs in your place of work should be a sacking offence. Be interesting to see what the creative director has to say.'

'He must condone it,' I said. 'It's so blatant. Unmistakeable. Oh, here's our stop. I'm off to pick up the Beamer and meet Arthur. Want to tag along?'

'Wouldn't miss it for all the coffee in Colombia.'

CHAPTER SIX

Buzz was waiting for us where we had parked the car the previous afternoon. From his white van, Arthur, carrying a towel, emerged to Buzz's disbelief. He simply stared transfixed at the man mountain ahead of him. Regaining his composure, if not awe, Buzz led us through the high-rise ghetto to the patch of concrete where ten boys and two girls awaited us.

'Who carries knives?' Arthur asked.

Five hands went up. One more than earlier. Our fame must be spreading.

'Form a line,' Arthur said. 'Those with knives at the front. I'm going to teach you defence, not attack.'

They did as he said. Who in their right mind was going to disobey him?

'I'm going to teach you to fight without a knife, because carrying a knife can so easily lead to death — one first step. You might kill, then end up on a murder charge and spend the rest of your life in prison. First, I'm going to teach you to fight against someone who is carrying a knife.'

He wound the towel around his left forearm. 'First boy,' he shouted. 'Come at me.'

The first boy in line hesitated. 'Come on,' Arthur said. 'I'm not going to hurt you. Attack me now.'

The boy ran at Arthur, the knife thrust forward. Arthur watched him, looking him straight in his eyes. As the boy approached, Arthur balanced himself, facing the boy full on. The boy thrust the knife at Arthur, who simply swept it aside with his protected left arm. That resulted in the boy spinning around and exposing himself to Arthur's defence. He grabbed the boy's right arm and twisted it up his back. The boy dropped the knife and stood there helpless.

'First lesson,' Arthur said, 'is to watch the eyes. That will tell you where the attack is coming from. Second lesson, use something, like in this case a towel, wrapped around your arm to use as protection. If you've got two towels or whatever, wrap the other one around the right forearm, just in case your attacker is left-handed. Next boy.'

The next boy obviously didn't want to do it, having seen how the boy before him had fared, and how easily Arthur had dealt with him. After a deep breath, the boy started to run at Arthur and swerved at the last moment. Arthur again swept the knife away, but this time, turned the boy 180 degrees and then locked his right forearm around the boy's neck.

'See,' he said. 'It can be so easy. You don't need a knife.'

'But,' said Buzz, who was next in line, 'you're massive. No one stands a chance against you.'

'Then try me,' I said. 'Come on, Buzz. I'm an easier opponent.'

'Do you really mean it?'

'No more talking. Come at me.'

I borrowed the towel and wrapped it the way Arthur had done. Buzz ran at me and I sidestepped. He couldn't face me anymore, so it was simple to chop at his right hand and he dropped the knife. I kicked it away and held his neck under my right arm. It was a long time since I had left myself so exposed. It felt good to feel that adrenalin rush again.

'I hear you say, what is the point of this?' I said. 'Apart from helping to keep you safe and out of prison, I have tasks for you all. When Arthur is happy with your progress, I will ask you follow certain people and report back to me everything you see. You'll get ten pounds for each session with Arthur, and twenty pounds plus travel expenses for every time you will report on them. Anyone want to bail out?'

Silence.

I slipped my hand inside my jacket pocket and took out a roll of ten-pound notes. I passed it to Anji. 'Do the honours,' I said.

She walked to the pack and dished out ten-pound notes, more than they had seen in a long while. 'I'll leave you in Arthur's capable hands.'

'Nick,' said Anji, 'I think I need to join the sessions. I can think of times when self-defence would have been lifesaving.'

'Agreed,' I said. 'Arthur will pick you up each day, same time. We should include Valentine, too. OK to wrap up here, Arthur? See you when you're done. Drop Anji off and join us all for a beer. Hasta . . . you know how it goes from there?'

* * *

I got home and placed the laptops on the long conference table in my office. I was tempted to start work on the accounts, but I'd had enough of Pym's for one day. I went into the river room and found Cherry there. 'All finished,' she said. 'I'll be available to you on Monday.'

'A drink to celebrate?' I asked, feeling a vodka and fresh orange juice calling.

'Just a diet cola with lots of ice,' she said. 'I'm so thirsty that I would glug a glass of white wine down without it touching the sides. How was your day?'

'I managed to antagonise a couple of people . . .'

'So situation normal there, then,' she said.

'Ha, ha,' I said. 'I met one of the most arrogant men I have come across for a long time.' I took a sip of my drink, and the world seemed a better place. 'I had a jingle composed for me which was designed to insult, and achieved it. What bothered me was that it might be true. Let's hope we meet some nicer people at tomorrow's fair. What should I wear? Any ideas?'

'I'm going for a sophisticated strapless dress gathered under my bosom and flowing to a pair of gold sandals. Can't risk heels, since we might spend our time walking on grass where they could dig in. If I were you, I would go for jeans, a T-shirt with a quirky design on it and a light-weight blouson jacket that can cope with the heat, if we're lucky enough to see some sun. But let's talk of happier things. I've arranged to see a possible venue on Sunday.'

'Venue?' I said.

'For our wedding, stupid,' she said. 'At the moment, they are available in two weeks due to a cancellation. Outside that, they're booked up for the next six months.'

'Gosh, that's quick,' I said. 'Will that allow us to make all the preparations?'

'We'll cross a few palms with silver,' she said.

'I haven't thought of who I'd want to invite.'

'I've already started work on that. In terms of a best man, I'd thought both Arthur and Norman could take on that duty — impossible to choose between the two — and escort you up the aisle. I'd like to pick Anji as maid of honour. I've seen a dress online, but I'll keep that secret. Don't want to have bad luck.'

'Where is this venue?' I said.

'Rural Essex. You'll love it. Stately pile going back centuries. Lots of atmosphere. We can even get married outside in the sunshine if the weather's clement. Oh, it's so exciting.'

Frightening might be a better word, but there was no sense in trying to change Cherry's mind. In two weeks we would be married, but there wasn't anything to object to. We would still be the same people, deeply in love with each other. A ring on a finger would be the only difference.

'A ring,' I said, panicking. 'What about a ring? Where can we get a ring?'

'Two rings, sweetheart,' she said. 'I'm not having you masquerading as a single man. There's a jewellers in Hatton Garden will make us up a pair. He owes me a favour from my time in the Fraud Squad and now's the time to collect. Trust me. It will all work out fine.'

'Take whatever time off you need,' I said, 'and make use of Morag and Beryl if you need to.' Then another thought entered my head. 'Honeymoon,' I said. 'What about a honeymoon?'

'I thought about the West Indies. I've got some brochures. I'll take you through them. Wait a moment.'

She left the room. I finished my drink and made another. Sipped rather than glugged this time. I had a feeling that it was going to be a long night.

CHAPTER SEVEN

It was a perfect day for the fete. There was a slight breeze and the late spring sun shone down like butterscotch and stuck to all my senses. Poetic, huh? Stolen, yes.

Pym had done its annual deal with a carnival travellers' band, and rides and attractions took up half of the three-acre fields. There was a spinning teacups, two bouncy castles, a see-saw type thing modelled as a boat with frightening height and a ghost train among them. The area at the other side of the site was set up with stalls selling a variety of home-made and artisan products, a beer tent and one selling tea and cakes. A hog turned slowly on a spit and there was the appetising smell of onions from a burger stand. For those with more exotic taste, there was a noodle bar. No expense had been spared.

There were the happy sounds from staff, clients and their families. There were men in shorts and flip-flops — never a pretty sight — and ladies wearing short white dresses or denim shorts, as if they had coordinated what to wear. Throughout them all, Pym circulated with a benevolent air. *Give them bread and circuses* flitted through my mind.

Cherry wore a long floaty dress with a print of poppies and low-heeled gold strappy sandals. I was wearing a pair of

37

sand chinos, a dark blue polo shirt, blue blouson jacket with matching loafers. Cool or what?

'Fancy a burger?' I said.

She looked at me disdainfully. 'A glass of Pimm's would seem appropriate,' she said.

We ambled over to the beer tent and bought two glasses of Pimm's — my only alcohol for the event since I was the designated driver and one who might have to revert to work mode — and stood in the sun sipping and listening to the happy cries of glee from children let off the leash. At a rough guess, I would have thought that there were around five hundred people there, including the children.

'Should we circulate?' she said.

'That's what we're here for,' I said. I looked around to see if there was anyone I had met at Pym's. The client I had talked to the other day, Matthew Bradley, stood watching the children thrilling at one of the bouncy castles. A good place to start.

He saw me and approached us, accompanied by a woman dressed in a white crop top and cut-off denim shorts that didn't seem to fit right for someone of her age and build. She had a pair of sunglasses on her head. Never a good sign, I thought, as I watched her squinting. He was wearing yellow chinos and a blue Hawaiian shirt so loud that it assaulted my eyes. Beneath the chinos peeked out a pair of sandals and socks — enough said.

We made the introductions — wife Sandra and son Billy bouncing away in a Spiderman outfit — and there was a moment of silence while we searched for a topic of conversation. Bradley stared at Cherry overlong and his wife scowled at him. I could sense a lecture — lecture for a lecher? — coming when they got home. Shame: it was what every man does when they first see Cherry. Impossible not to be transfixed.

'Is that Pimm's?' Bradley said. 'Must be the drink of the day, eh? Pimm's and Pym's, you know?'

'Billy!' Sandra screamed like an actor in Eastenders. My eardrums exploded. 'Don't do that.' She turned to us.

'Good to get out of the house for some good clean family fun. Matthew would sit in front of the telly all day if you let him.'

'It's part of my job,' he said. 'I need to see what the competition is doing.' He turned to me and said, 'What did you make of Tony and Ned yesterday? Odd couple, eh? You wouldn't think they could work as a team, would you? Tony is a real gourmet, too. Always treats me to some fine meals. Ned never eats anything but bloody steaks. Caveman style.'

'Sums him up in one meal,' I said. 'I get the impression that they could push you to the limit just for the fun of it.'

'They're not so bad once you get to know them. You got them on a bad day — that supermarket ad to do. Maybe once you get to know them better, they will be less antagonistic.'

'Nick is a detective,' Bradley explained to his wife. 'Fraud. Must like a puzzle.'

'How old is Billy?' Cherry asked, trying to see if we could find out anything by following the family route.

'He's just turned seven,' Sandra said. 'Big boy for his age.'

'Any other children?' Cherry probed.

'Just one daughter. Fourteen. Typical teenager. All she does is grunt and sulk.'

Not too different from Ned, then, I thought.

'Children can be so expensive,' Cherry said. 'How are the schools near you?'

'We've put them in a private school. We both agree that it's a good investment for the future. Won't be long before uni. That's going to hit the wallet, too.'

'What with house prices going up and up,' Cherry said, 'it can be a struggle getting the home you want. What would be your dream home?'

'Somewhere by the sea,' she said. 'Walks along the beach each morning. Great view from the living room … but that's just a dream. We're stuck where we are at the moment. Unless Matthew gets a promotion at last, we're in limbo where we are. That's how life goes. Right, Matthew? You promised to take me and Billy on the ghost train. Everybody heard you. There's no getting out of it. See you later,' she said to us.

'What did you think of Sandra?' I said to Cherry. 'Apart from the fact that she shouldn't wear denim jeans and a crop top.'

'That's the size one gets after a child or two. You really need to assess your wardrobe and chuck out anything that is going to be skin-tight. I wonder if his salary is enough to run to a gym, or better still, a private trainer. Wish I'd asked now, but she seemed in a rush to move on.'

'That's the Cherry factor,' I said. 'Jealousy, plus the desire to get the man elsewhere before he starts drooling.'

To my sinking stomach, I saw Tony Lancaster heading in our direction. He was wearing beige moleskin trousers like you see in catalogues for the older man. Coordinated, he had on a beige shirt, cuffs turned over and could have been going on safari. A sheepish man followed in his wake, seemingly unsure as to what he was supposed to do — to faint sounded a good option. If Tony started jibes about Cherry or inappropriate jingles, I might sock him in the bronzed face. A punch-up might be the first in the history of the fair.

'So who have we here?' he said.

'Significant other,' I said.

'Fiancée,' said Cherry.

'Fiancée,' I corrected myself. 'Goes by the name of Cherry.'

'Well, pleased to meet you, Cherry. I must say that Shannon has a great taste in women. You're a lucky man, Shannon. What do you do, Cherry? How did your paths cross?'

'I work with him,' she said. 'I'm ex-Fraud Squad. We met there many moons ago.'

'And you've been together all these years without getting married? How could he resist for so long?'

'Like all things, the past can be murky,' she said. 'Nick has told me all about you.'

'Unfortunately, it will all be true,' he said. 'How remiss of me.' He turned to the sheepish man. 'This is my friend Nigel. He's a fair virgin, finding it all a bit mystifying. Aren't you, Nigel?'

Nigel nodded.

Lancaster seemed to attach himself to people who, in his company, lost their ability to speak. Maybe they'd just given up on trying to get a word in edgewise. Lancaster went in more for soliloquies rather than dialogue.

We were interrupted, thankfully, by the arrival of Sir Gerald Campion. 'Great to see you again, Cherry,' he said. He took her hand and kissed it. 'How is it going with Pym's?' he said to me.

'Only just started,' I said. 'Early days. I have a feeling it's going to be more complex than we initially thought. Just a gut feeling that I can't explain. Pym seems a good man, though, and we've got his full backing. I'll keep you posted. Tony here is one of the copywriters. Maybe he'll write a jingle for you.'

'I would hate to hear it,' Campion said, 'No historic deeds, and I dread to think of my present situation.'

'Champion rhymes with Campion,' Tony said. 'I'll work on it.'

'I'll leave you before we start talking business,' said Campion. 'Enjoy this fine weather. Perfect day for the fair. If there's anything I can do, Nick, just let me know.'

He drifted off around the circumference of the fields.

'That was Sir Gerald Campion?' Lancaster said. 'You move in exalted circles, Shannon. I might just have to start being nice to you. Come along, Nigel. Places to go, people to see.'

'What an odious person,' Cherry said, when they were gone.

'And that's his good side,' I said. 'How much more time do you think we should stay for politeness?'

'One lap around the fields,' Cherry said.

We set off going past the spinning cups and saw Bradley and crew arrive at the head of the queue for the ghost train.

We moved closer to the black tunnel that composed the ride — frightening in the dark for children with scary figures and animals, bats and black cats popping up out of the gloom — and watched the three of them, wife and child squeezed beside him into a car built for two. They disappeared on the rail that led the car round the attraction into the blackness.

A moment later, it seemed, I heard a scream. A pitch so high that it chilled me.

There, in the car, was Bradley. With a knife sticking out of his chest.

I ran towards them and took in the scene at first glance. Whoever had done it had sliced across his stomach first and then stuck the dagger in his chest.

'Phone 999, Walker,' I said. 'Ambulance and police. Then phone DI Palmer. Then do what you can for Sandra and Billy.'

Billy was covered in blood and sat there in the train in stunned silence, stiff as a board. Sandra was there next to him screaming without break.

The attendant ran over, and together we lifted Bradley out of the car and laid him on the grass. I left the knife in, unsure whether leaving it in or pulling it out was the best course of action. I took off my jacket, rolled it up and pressed it on the stomach wound to try to stop the blood that was pouring out. In my heart of hearts, I knew it was a forlorn hope, but couldn't think of anything else to do. It was a lost cause. In truth, I didn't know how he had lasted this long. My jacket was now soaked with blood, but I couldn't give up on the futile cause.

Cherry had got Sandra and Billy out of the car and had huddled them together so that she could hug both of them at the same time. One of the stall holders had brought over two chairs and sat them down. Sandra was, naturally, totally hysterical. She pulled Billy across and on to her lap.

I didn't know what was the response time for the police and ambulance to arrive was, but it would be too late. I then realised that I had made a mistake by focusing exclusively on Bradley rather than at the ghost train. Whoever had stabbed him would have slipped away unnoticed.

There was now a crowd watching us, seemingly gaining some puerile fascination from the event. Bradley opened his eyes and looked at me. 'McLuhan,' he said, and stopped breathing.

I heard sirens screaming. Police? Ambulance? Both? Too late. I closed his eyes and stood up. Campion came across to me. 'Who was the fellow?' he said.

'Client,' I said. 'Brand manager for Seeco crisps. God knows why someone would do this to him.'

'I'll find Pym,' said Campion. 'Break the bad news. I'll see if we can put someone on the gate to stop anyone leaving before the police arrive. I must say, Nick, that you seem to have a knack of magnetically attracting murders. You must let me know, some time — what is your secret?'

It was just a little bit later, no more than ten minutes although it seemed a lifetime, when DI Dennis Palmer arrived. He was six feet tall and wearing his customary off-the-peg grey suit and white shirt with a red tie. I had always thought that his wife chose his clothes, and this suit had lasted for many years. The jacket didn't do up over his barrel chest, but because of his OCD, everything he wore had not one crease in sight.

'Welcome, DI Palmer,' I said, 'although I wish it was under better circumstances.'

'It's DCI Palmer now,' he said. 'Thanks to you helping me solve a murder and close down a drugs ring. I think the wife is quite pleased that I'm not retiring yet, and won't be getting under her feet the whole time. I must say that I'm not totally surprised to see you here. Dead bodies seem to follow you around. What can you tell me?'

'The victim was Matthew Bradley, brand manager at Seeco.'

'The crisps business?' he said.

'The same,' I said.

'What's a brand manager do?'

'Manages the brand,' I said. 'Whatever that means. From what I have experienced so far, I think it means keeping everybody on track with the overall message coming from the brand. Probably involves strategy as well. Apart from that, you're as wise as I am.'

He walked over to the body, which was now inside crime scene tape, and where a tent was being erected. He stood back from it and asked for some shoe coverings for both of us, so as to protect the area from being compromised. He took in the obvious knife sticking out of the victim's chest and lifted off my jacket from the body.

'Whoever did this,' Palmer said, 'wasn't taking any chances. Either wound was enough to kill him. Both was overkill. Did you touch the body?'

'Only to lift him out of the train and to press my jacket over the stomach wound. I didn't touch the knife, although I don't think you will get any prints off it. For a killer this careful, it was almost certain that he or she would have worn gloves and wiped the knife clean, too.'

'Clever way to kill someone,' Palmer said. 'The killer would be concealed in the darkness waiting for this Bradley man and slipped away in the confusion that took place when the ride finished. Man or woman, do you think?'

'Man,' I said. 'Poison is a woman's method.'

'Expert on murder now as well as fraud?'

'I read a lot,' I said. 'You should try it.'

'And when am I going to find the time, with you calling me every five minutes with a new corpse?'

'It's not that often,' I said.

He looked me straight in the eye.

'OK,' I said. 'It is getting quite frequent.'

He kept his gaze on me.

'Let's say very frequent then,' I said.

'That's about right,' he said. 'Anything else you can tell me?'

'Lots of people apparently heard him promise to take his wife and Billy, his son, on the ghost train, so the net of possible killers is wide. He did say something strange with his last breath.'

'And?'

'He said just the one word. "McLuhan".'

'What does that mean?' Palmer said.

'I haven't a clue. Worth following up, though. If you know you only have one breath left, you can't go into a long declamation of the killer. Must be important. I suppose it's possible he didn't know his killer. Hit man? We need to do the usual things — search his home and confiscate any computers.'

'Can I remind you that now is not the time for grand-mothers to be told about sucking eggs, Shannon?'

'Just thinking aloud, Palmer,' I said.

'Let's get the wife and kid home,' he said. 'Then I must interview her as soon as possible. Want to tag along?'

'I'd be honoured,' I said.

'Well, you've proved useful in the past and, I suppose, I owe you one. Let's tidy up here and then get on our way.'

I followed him to where Sandra sat with a uniformed female officer bending over her. Cherry stood directly behind them. She saw me coming and walked over to me.

'Bad business,' she said, holding me tight. 'Always ter-rible to lose a loved one, but this is not like he was dying of cancer or something. This is just premeditated murder, and in the most brutal form.'

'Palmer — DCI now — is going to interview Sandra and start a search of their home. Her home now, I suppose. I'm going to go with him. Take the Beamer and have a large brandy when you get back. I'll phone Norman and tell him the situation. Once you're home, the shock will kick in. Better stay off the coffee for a while and try to rest.'

'Will do,' she said. 'Such a terrible thing. What a way to go.'

'You do know what this means, don't you?'

'Tell me.'

'The share price of Pym's has just tanked.'

45

CHAPTER EIGHT

Bradley's house was a three-storey town house south of the river. It was set among identical three-storey townhouses that had no individualities or charm. Soulless. Little boxes, as the song goes. A sacrifice for school fees. A long way from Sandra's dream of a place by the sea. There was a ten-year-old Ford Fiesta in the driveway. Just about sums it all up. Get the picture? I didn't like it.

The police community officer offered tea, which we accepted, as much to do with joining Sandra as any thirst we might have had. She was sitting huddled up on a dark brown two-seater sofa with big padded arms that made the room look smaller. Another two-seater sofa and a faux-leather tan recliner were lined up pointed at the TV. There were toys tidily put away in clear plastic crates. There was no sign of Billy.

Palmer got the session going with the stupid question that had to be answered for politeness as much as anything else. 'How are you feeling, Sandra?'

'Numb,' she said. 'I can't believe it. Who would want to kill Matthew? He didn't have any enemies. He was just an ordinary bloke. There's no reason why someone would want him dead.'

46

'What about work?' I said. 'Any rivalries there?'

'No,' she said firmly. 'He wasn't a threat to anyone. He was happy with what he was doing. We both knew he wouldn't get further up the ladder. He wasn't promotion material. He'd got as far as he was going up the greasy pole.'

'Where's Billy?' I asked.

'Grandparents. How do I explain this to him — and my daughter? Got no dad anymore. He must be in trauma. Sitting next to Matthew when he was stabbed to death. He's not said a word since then. Speechless. PTSD, I suppose you'd call it. My daughter will probably go that way, too.'

She looked so vulnerable sitting on the sofa in her crop top and denim shorts that I wanted to scoop her up and give her a big hug. But there was worse to come. Whoever had killed Bradley must have two children on their conscience as well, if they had a conscience, that is.

The cups of tea arrived and I watched Palmer put three heaped spoonfuls in his. The woman officer, Katy, sat next to Sandra. There was no way that Sandra could manage to drink her tea as she would just spill it because her hands were shaking so much. I went through to the kitchen and found a bigger mug. The kitchen, much like everything I had seen so far, was tired and ordinary — drawings on the fridge door, cork board for admin things like party invitations, doctors' appointments and so on. While I was there, I used the first opportunity I'd had to wash the blood from my hands. I watched it swirl around the sink and down the plughole as if everything was over. No blood on my hands anymore. I hoped that was an omen. I went back to the living room and poured the cup of tea into the larger mug. Handed it to her and she managed a small smile. Progress?

'Any problems with the neighbours?' Palmer said, scratching around for any clue. 'Anyone got any grudges against him that you know of? Boundary disputes, loud music from here, that sort of thing?'

Sandra shook her head. 'Nothing. He wouldn't hurt a flea. The most gentle of men.'

'What about his relationship with Pym's? Anything that would trouble him there?' I asked, realising I was doing Palmer's work for him, but he was looking around the room, taking it all in and resisting the temptation to make everything line up straight.

'I'm sorry to have to ask, but we'll need to search his laptop or computer and any papers that he had,' Palmer said. 'I know it's not the best time, but every minute we lose, the murderer gets further away and the less chance we have of finding him or her.'

'Go ahead,' Sandra said. 'It's not that I'm going any-where. Matthew used a desk in our bedroom for work things and everyday paperwork, bank statements and such.'

'So Pym's?' I said, to make doubly sure. 'Any problems there? Anyone that he might have upset there?'

'He got on well with everyone there,' Sandra said. 'He found it exciting watching the process towards a finished ad, and he loved seeing the commercial. I can't really say any-thing about the people he dealt with there. He didn't bring his work home, one of the advantages of being settled in his job. He didn't have to do any overtime.'

'I have to ask,' I said, 'but did he have anything to do with drugs?'

'You didn't mention anything about that,' Palmer said sharply.

'It's just that I smelled something I think was weed in the office of the creative team,' I said. 'It's only now that it's come into my mind. Probably nothing to it.'

'He wouldn't have anything to do with drugs,' Sandra said. 'He was a sensible man. A family man. He was a bit addicted to the TV, you could say, but that's as far as it goes. Didn't drink to excess or smoke. He wouldn't have done any-thing so foolish as drugs, nothing to jeopardise us as a family.'

'If you don't mind.' Palmer said, 'we'll have a look upstairs. We'll try not to disturb anything.'

We placed our empty cups on the tray Katy had brought in. Palmer looked like it was sacrilege not to be able to put his cup on a drip mat or saucer. I wondered how much use he would be combing through everything.

We went upstairs and found a small desk in front of a window in the master bedroom. It was a small room, but the desk didn't impinge too much. I guessed the house was too small, not enough bedrooms to allow him an office of his own. The bedroom walls were painted a pastel shade of pink and there was a small double bed with cabinets each side. On one of the cabinets there was a radio and a pair of headphones, on the other was a paperback book of detective fiction. I wondered which side was which. Palmer went through the cabinets while I tackled the desk. There was a pile of papers to the left of a laptop. Within the pile were bank statements. I leafed through them before, presumably with Palmer's permission, a more detailed examination; they might have had the first clue to follow up.

The statements showed that finances were healthy, no overdraft needed or signs of penury. I looked more closely at them and called Palmer over.

'Look at this,' I said. 'Every month a cash, repeat untraceable cash, deposit of two thousand pounds. From what I can tell, this has been going on for around six months. I suspect it was meant that Bradley must keep his mouth shut. Over what? Who knows? Maybe he wanted more of the action, whatever that was, and someone went for silencing him on a more permanent basis.'

'We may have discovered a motive,' Palmer said. 'We'll go back to your place and you can download everything to a hard disk and take copies of all the paperwork. I don't know when we'll get a chance for a detailed look at everything, bearing in mind tomorrow is Sunday, so you'll be a day or so ahead of us. That way I can officially hand everything in. I'm only doing this because in the past you've managed to dig up vital evidence. You've got a nose for spotting things that we don't have. You keep me posted the moment you have any progress.'

'I'm getting the feeling that something here is connected to Pym's,' I said. 'I don't know if we will still have a job on Monday

— Bradley's murder throws everything in doubt — but, if we do, I'll continue my interviews with the key staff. You'll probably have to do the same, but maybe I can point you in the right direction and save you some time and inconvenience.'

I turned on the laptop and, helpfully, found it wasn't password-protected. There were icons at the bottom of the screen for Word and Excel, so that was promising. A quick look at the most recently used files in File Manager let me see that everything was neatly stored in labelled folders. That should decrease the time to be spent on trawling through all the material. I was hopeful, but had my fingers crossed. Can't do any harm.

The desk drawers had nothing useful, just a collection of stationery and business cards from tradesmen — plumbers, electricians and the like. There was a double wardrobe along one wall and I opened the doors more out of habit than thinking I might find something pertinent. Inside, Sandra's clothes took up two-thirds of the space and Matthew's the remaining third. They certainly were not spendthrifts. There weren't any expensive designer clothes or racks of shoes. Matthew's side contained three dark blue suits and around ten shirts of many colours with white, pale blue and a rebellious pink being predominant.

'Discover anything?' Palmer asked, as he was looking underneath the mattress.

'They weren't living beyond their means, although I suspect we will find that school fees might be responsible for living close to the edge on the spending front. They're borderline, but not desperate for money. I'll reserve judgement until I've had a detailed look.'

'Seen enough?' Palmer said.

I nodded my head.

'One last look at the living room and then we can leave,' he said.

We bundled up the papers and the laptop and went downstairs. Katy was sitting beside Sandra, holding her hand. Sandra was still shaking.

'Finished upstairs, sir?' Katy said. 'I'd like to get Sandra to her bedroom to change out of these clothes and into something different, you know?'

You know was important.

There were a few splashes of blood on the crop top, but I reckoned Billy had come out worse from the spurting of the wound on his stomach. He would never forget this day, and would need a lot of counselling if he was to recover from the mental scars. PTSD was a certainty. Poor kid. I wondered how his sister would cope. A bad age for something like this — but, I suppose, there is never a good age.

'We'll be off in a moment,' Palmer said. 'If you need any backup, just call the station.'

Katy helped Sandra out of the chair and led her up the stairs. I went to the low table on which to stand the TV and opened the doors to see if there were any clues inside. The cupboards contained a range of DVDs, a chess set, Scrabble, a pack of cards and a set of poker chips to liven up the family games. I went to the recliner and sat on it to see whether it was comfortable enough for a long session watching TV. It fitted the bill. On the floor beside the chair was a programme guide with circles around the planned viewing, mostly cosy crime, thrillers and a few cooking shows. That told me little about his personality, apart from he went for the popular shows and didn't need to extend his brain too much.

We gathered up everything and left the house. On the journey back to Docklands, nothing was said. I hoped someone would catch the murderer and bring forth some justice and closure for the family. I wasn't optimistic.

* * *

When we arrived back we found everybody in the river room. Against my instructions, Cherry was drinking a latte while the others had full glasses of restorative alcohol. She had stopped shaking, so had made some progress.

I sent Anji into my office to start copying everything on Bradley's laptop and Valentine to copy all the paperwork. Palmer went through discreetly to watch them, but probably to give Cherry and I some privacy. Norman, Morag and Beryl, so not to get in our way, went upstairs with their drinks.

'I thought,' said Cherry, 'that my years as a copper had shown me all that life could hit me with — do you remember that case while you were seconded to the Fraud Squad? The man who jumped out of the window of the skyscraper; the mess his body was in? But this is worse. Someone must be very deranged to do this to a body. It's so calculated. So full of hate.'

'They most important thing at the moment,' I said, 'is you. How are you feeling?'

'Numb,' she said.

I went across to where Cherry was sitting on one of the sofas and promptly sat down beside her. I put an arm around her and pulled her close.

'Who could do such a thing?' she said. 'It's sadistic. Someone who gets a kick out of killing in the most despicable way.'

'If it is any consolation, and I know that events so sad cannot be any consolation, but we were not the victims. It's possible that it isn't connected to our work at Pym's, but we should watch out in the future. I'll get Arthur to ride shotgun on us till the job is over.'

'I'm not so convinced that there isn't a link with Pym's,' Cherry said. 'Seems too coincidental. Maybe we should bow out gracefully before something else happens. I know what you're going to say, so I expect I'm talking to a deaf ear.'

'We have signed a contract, so we must complete it. To give in now would be without honour. Promises must be kept.'

'As I said, deaf ear,' she said. 'Oh, what a silly woman I am. How stupid. Let's get absorbed in Pym's and finish it within a week or so.'

'If Vernon Pym wants us to continue, that is,' I said. 'This puts the whole job in a different light, puts a different complexion on this. The share price may have dropped so much as to make the sale unviable. Which clients and potential clients will want to work through Pym's? Safety must be a factor in their minds.'

I topped up my drink and walked around the room. The river shone with the imminent arrival of sunset and all seemed at peace.

'Anji and Valentine,' Cherry said, 'can work together tomorrow while we go to see the venue. You hadn't forgot about seeing the venue in the morning, had you?'

'Of course not,' I lied. 'Be a nice break after today. Something to take our minds off events and we can give the Beamer a run. Maybe stop at a nice country pub for a full English brunch.'

Palmer walked back in with the laptop and papers. 'Anyone want to talk about the elephant in the room?' he said.

'We've already talked about it,' I said. 'Our view is that the murder might not be anything to do with Pym's.'

'The important word is *might*,' he said. 'I didn't think you went in for wishful thinking, Shannon. Why do you think I'm involving you in this investigation? That's right. I think you've done your regular job as acting as a catalyst. Your contract with Pym's has stirred something up. Someone wants your contract cancelled before you find the rotten apple in the barrel. Sounds familiar, doesn't it?'

'And your advice?' I said.

'Watch your backs.'

CHAPTER NINE

Cherry was much less despondent on Sunday morning as we drove to some rural pile in the backwoods of Essex. Her normal smile was back on her face. She may have not got over Bradley's murder — there would need to be much more talking and reflection before that — but she had started the mending process. The atmosphere had softened as the Beamer purred along the country miles.

It was impressive, I had to say that for it. It was the sort of place that should be owned by the National Trust, since its upkeep was probably exorbitant, but, as a thriving business, maybe it was keeping its head above the listed building category with all the added expense that goes with it. The brochure we had been given stated that parts of the building went back as far as the sixteenth century. The biggest question was why. Why build a mansion so remote and far from civilisation? Purely, a place to retreat to when danger erupts. It seemed so fitting today.

There was a long sweeping drive and a place for parking around the back where it would not affect the tranquillity of the front view. The central building was four storeys high and then, so the brochure again informed me, two additional wings at its flanks were constructed mid-seventeenth century.

We parked the Beamer around the back and watched as Arthur's van pulled into the space beside us.

'No problems,' he said. 'No one following. Clean as a whistle. What a gaff! What a place to get married.'

'It's everything I dreamed of,' said Cherry. 'This is going to be spectacular.'

'I'll take a walk around the grounds while you're getting the guided tour,' Arthur said. 'Keep my eyes on comings and goings, too.'

Cherry and I walked round the building and pulled an antique lion's head that reverberated deeply to signal our arrival. We were greeted by a young woman of late twenties with precise make-up and wearing a smart navy-blue trouser suit with an RAF-blue blouse. She introduced herself as Sheila and guided us to a large oak desk with a patina of many hands rubbing it over the ages. She gave us brochures for all the necessary tradespeople who would add the finishes touches to the wedding — photographers, hairdresser and the like. From there, she led us up a wide staircase to the second floor. There, in all its glory, was the room where we were to get married.

'Let's assume the weather is not good enough for the ceremony to be held outside,' Sheila said. 'This is where you would have the ceremony indoors. How many guests are you thinking of?'

'It won't be large,' Cherry said. 'Maybe fifty.'

Fifty! That was far more than I had thought. Outside Arthur and Norman and the team, I didn't have any other friends apart from Sir Gerald, our computer guy Canning and Martin, our lawyer. Where are all the others coming from?

'There will be a lot of police invited,' Cherry said, answering my unspoken question. 'So you shouldn't have any trouble.'

'In my experience,' Sheila said, 'policeman can be the most trouble. Get a few beers inside them and then all hell breaks loose.'

We stood at the back of the room counting seats, but there would be plenty to go round.

'You'll progress up the aisle to the end — lots of photo opportunities — and come to rest before the lectern. This is where the registrar will stand to conduct the marriage ceremony. Let's talk sashes,' she said. 'All the chairs will have white cloth over them. To make them look more attractive we tie sashes across the backs. There's a choice of twenty-five different colourways. Let me show you.'

I was already reeling from the shock of a choice of twenty-five sashes. I had the feeling that this was going to be done with military precision. And that the pub meal wasn't going to fit into the schedule.

Sheila led us to a framed exhibition of all the colours tied neatly in little bows.

'They're all so sweet,' said Cherry. 'What do you think, Nick?'

'All so sweet,' I said. 'Can't choose between them.'

'I'm torn between two of them. What do you think, Nick?'

'The navy-blue one would complement your eyes.'

'Too dull,' Cherry said, in afterthought. 'What about the turquoise one?'

'Excellent choice,' I said.

Sheila jotted it down on her clipboard. 'We'll look outside in a moment, but while we're on this floor, I'll show you some of the rooms.'

We followed her along a narrow corridor into a large room with a four-poster bed and a full-length mirror. The walls were a blush pink and there were architraves and central roses that spoke of years long ago. The lower part of the walls was wood going back centuries. Dominating the room was a grand four-poster bed.

'This is the bride's room,' Sheila said, 'and where the two of you will spend the night. Notice what a lovely lot of photo opportunities there are. Imagine how you will feel standing in front of the mirror, full make-up done, hair coiffed and in a long wedding gown. What colour dress are you going for?'

'White. Pure white. This wedding will be a rebirth, an epiphany. Everything must be perfect.'

'And this is the groom's room,' Sheila said.

The room was smaller than the bride's room, but still had a four-poster bed and all the trimmings of yesteryear. Fittingly, the walls were a light blue and had a relaxed feel that might come in handy for any last-minute jitters, not that I was expecting any. Well, not many. I would only be here in order to get dressed for the ceremony — light grey made-to-measure suit, if time, and a pale blue striped shirt.

The mansion had eight further bedrooms that we whizzed around. That should be sufficient for our team, including Toddy, and one for Sir Gerald, who would be the least mobile of the guests.

Sheila took us down the stairs and into the vast room where the wedding breakfast would be served. More sashes. But who could condemn more sashes? Cherry chose a light pink. Fine by me. It would be Cherry's day and she could have anything she wanted.

Sheila sat us down on the long table which would be for the guests of honour — that word again. Honour. There were two places set up ready for us and Sheila poured a glass of chilled white wine and another of red.

'These are our house wines,' Sheila said. 'Very popular, although we could accommodate any other wines of your choice.'

'We'll bring our own,' I said. There was no way that Norman would get any appreciation from the thin wines of the house. 'The white will need to be chilled and the red opened the day before so it can breathe.'

'We'll have to charge corkage,' Sheila said.

The booze would be where a large slice of the money for the wedding was made. Fair enough. I nodded.

A young girl dressed in black and white — that's how they got their name, I suppose — brought in a tray with a variety of food in small dishes and lids.

'We can plan menus to suit your preferences and we always provide vegan dishes.' She lifted a dish containing rare roast beef. 'We find this is one of our most popular dishes, although the ladies prefer our salmon with a Chinese glaze.'

Voilà. The cover was lifted and there was the salmon. It was cooked almost perfectly — we couldn't expect anything like Toddy's standard — maybe a bit too pink for some guests. Passable.

There were examples of starters and desserts, all on a list of possible choices, with selections of vegetables. I went back to the beef and took a bite of the Yorkshire pudding that came with the beef. Grudgingly, it was good, light, crisp — Toddy would approve.

'Shall we decide now?' Cherry said.

'Might as well,' I said. 'One more thing done and dusted.'

'We'll have the assorted salamis and hams to start,' she said, 'followed by the beef and salmon. Wedding cake to finish — no dessert.'

'Good,' Sheila said. 'I'll show you the all-important bar next. Did you want a cash bar, or fully paid bar, with all drinks free throughout the evening.'

'Free throughout,' I said, making my first choice of the visit, although it would be fine with me if Cherry countermanded it. I was starting to get the jitters. This was so important to Cherry — nothing must be short of perfection.

'We'll have the fireworks at eight,' Sheila said, 'and the buffet immediately after: casseroles, fried chicken, sausages, all the usual things — we'll choose for you from our favourites.'

The bar was a large room with a long bar in shiny oak in keeping with the olde-worlde tradition. There was a ten-foot circle picked out in floor lights for dancing, and tables for sitting down and watching the action. It was here I would be having the first dance — I would need some lessons if not to make a fool of myself.

Finally, it was time to go outside. There was a small white pergola for the couple and a marquee for the guests to shelter in if the weather became inclement. It was staggeringly beautiful with the backdrop of the lawns and the surrounding trees. Many photos would be taken here.

'We'll plan for an outside wedding,' said Cherry. 'So romantic — but move inside if the weather is against us.'

Time for the paperwork. To confirm the deal.

Sheila took us back inside and sat us down in her office where the vital card reader was waiting for us. I paid a twenty per cent deposit and Cherry held on to my arm. 'So exciting,' she said. 'It's all going to be like a dream.'

We shook hands to seal the contract and left. Arthur was standing by his van, looking around.

'Well,' I said. 'What do you think of the place?'

'Don't like it,' he said. 'Too many trees. If I was planning a battle, I wouldn't fight it here.'

'It's good we're here for a wedding and not a war,' Cherry said sharply.

'Sorry,' he said. 'Old habits die hard.'

"Who is going to give you away?' I said to Cherry.

'I don't have any family,' she said. 'I'm thinking of Palmer, and then Anji as maid of honour. What do you think of that?'

'Palmer will be thrilled,' I said, 'and Anji would be the best support you could have.'

'I'll start phoning all the other key people tomorrow,' she said. 'It's going to be unforgettable.'

* * *

We arrived back to find Anji and Valentine deep in examination of the accounts and the copies of Bradley's paperwork, respectively. There was a plate of sandwiches and some cans of Red Bull on the table.

'Are you finished with the sandwiches?' I asked hopefully.

'Go ahead,' Valentine said. 'All lovingly fresh prepared by Beryl.'

Cherry and I sat down and each picked up a sandwich — smoked salmon and horseradish. It was beyond good.

'How did you get on with the wedding venue?' Anji asked.

'Couldn't have made a better choice if we'd tried,' Cherry said. 'We need to decide on what colour of dress you want to wear as my maid of honour.'

'Maid of honour? Me? That's so wonderful. I'd be delighted. How about blue? That always works well with my blonde hair and blue eyes. I don't want to upstage you.'

'Let's go shopping tomorrow,' Cherry said. 'Spend, spend, spend. How much cash do we have in the safe, if I need a sweetener for the dresses or to grease the palm of the photographer and the others?'

'Plenty,' I said. 'Take what you need. I'll take Valentine with me to Pym's. If we still have a job, that is.'

'I've been looking at Bradley's paperwork,' Valentine said. 'It's all pretty normal until four months ago, then we get the cash deposits. That, in itself, looks suspicious. Untraceable. Smells like blackmail to my untrained mind. Bradley was on to something. I don't know what, but I'll keep digging.'

'Good work, Valentine,' I said. 'Keep on it for the moment. Maybe something will turn up. Have you tried looking at where the cash goes? Second bank account? Was he planning a moonlight flit? Anything to indicate he was off for sunnier climes? Can you tell anything about how he gets on with his wife?'

'Nothing suspicious. He takes her out for a meal regularly after the monthly cash arrives. Same restaurant, same bill amount. Man of habit. Or it might be someone else he takes out, I suppose. Sounds more like a treat away from the kids, for everything they put into the family. In a word — normal.'

'Any luck with his laptop, Anji?' I asked.

'Basically, the usual housekeeping — spreadsheets to keep control of his bank account and credit cards — he pays off the balance in full each month — list of direct debits with amounts of each, scans of his driving licence, utility bill and passport, presumably all the ID information you need to open a bank account. Nothing in his emails to warrant further examination. His internet history doesn't suggest he was into porn or gambling. They're jogging along, financially — not much money in the bank, but they're not strapped for money, either.'

'I took a break out of boredom,' said Anji, 'and had a quick look at some of the accounts for Pym's. What is it you said about suspense accounts?'

'What is it I said about suspense accounts?' I asked. 'Words of wisdom, obviously.'

'You said a suspense account should be a last resort, if you can't decide where money should go in the accounts. You said small amounts, and for no more than a month.'

'As I said — words of wisdom. Why?'

'Pym's has got a million pounds in the suspense account, and has had for the last three months.'

'Wow,' I said. 'That sounds decidedly fishy. We might have found a reason for the contract not to be cancelled. We'll grill O'Hara first thing tomorrow. We could be back in business. I smell a bonus for us.'

'What a perfect day,' said Cherry. 'Absolutely perfect! Just what I needed. I can smell a celebration in the air.'

Don't count your chickens, Cherry, I thought.

CHAPTER TEN

If the word *bland* had to be invented, then it would be because of needing a word to describe O'Hara. He was dressed in a black suit with a white shirt. The tie today was plain black. No lion today. Maybe that was the unconventional done for the year, or maybe it was brought on to mark Bradley's passing.

The mood at Pym's was sombre, partly because of the loss of a long-time client who would be sadly missed by those who dealt with him, and partly due to fear. Would the killer strike again and, if so, who would be the next victim? The sword of Damocles was hanging over heads. Everyone was looking up.

Valentine and I organised ourselves in our office, logging into the accounts package and making one final check of the suspense account and walked upstairs to O'Hara's office. When we entered, his face fell. He knew that we knew. There was no point in beating about the proverbial bush.

'There's a million pounds in the suspense account,' I said. 'Tell us about it.'

'Our soft drinks client, Phantom, was nearly at its year end. They were underspent against budget for the year. That meant that the parent company would cut their budget for the following year. They asked us to bill them early before the year end, meaning they would avoid a budget cut. We duly obliged and billed them one million pounds in advance. That's why I put the figure in the suspense account. Simple, really.'

'And where is this money now?' I asked. 'I can't see it in sales.'

'I invested it, so we would make some money instead of it just sitting in the bank, earning close to zero interest.'

'What did you invest it in?' I said.

'I spread the money over a range of stocks across the world — the UK, American, Japan, Hong Kong and so on — so as to minimise the risks.'

I felt like I was pulling teeth. Lots of questions, little answers.

'So what is the value of the stocks now?' I said, hoping to get a straight answer.'

'Eight hundred thousand pounds,' he said.

'You made eight hundred thousand pounds?' I said. 'Well done.' I relaxed a bit.

'No,' he said, 'the value of the portfolio is eight hundred thousand pounds. The stock markets were against me. Bought at the wrong time, but stock markets will recover over the long term.'

My heart dropped.

'But this isn't going to be long term,' I said. 'How soon will the client want to spend the money?'

'We've got a month or so,' he said.

'And you think the stock markets are going to go up by twenty-five per cent over the next month or so? You're not only optimistic, but deluded. Does Pym know about this?'

'No,' he said. 'I thought I'd surprise him when I told him what I'd done.'

'Instead of surprise, it's going to be a shock,' I said. 'I think you need to bite the bullet and give him the bad news. Gather yourself, O'Hara. Let's go.'

O'Hara, Valentine and I walked along the corridor and found Brookie acting as sentinel. She knocked on his door and we went in without waiting for an answer.

'This is not a good time,' Pym said.

'Oh, how right you are,' I said.

'You better sit down,' Pym said. 'I need to talk to you about your contract anyway, Shannon.'

'O'Hara has some bad news,' I said. 'Over to you, O'Hara. Spill the beans, as they say.'

'It's a long story,' O'Hara said. 'You know that million pounds Phantom asked to bill. Well, I invested it. I spread over a range of stocks over several countries, so as . . .'

'For goodness' sake,' I said, my patience wearing thin. 'Let's cut to the chase, to use an overdone phrase. He's lost you two hundred thousand pounds.'

Pym slumped back in his chair. 'I don't understand.'

'O'Hara invested it and the markets went belly up on him,' I said, making a mental note not to resort to any more clichés. 'You're two hundred grand out of pocket.' Did that count as a cliché?

'What do you propose we do?' Pym said to O'Hara.

O'Hara shrugged. Not the best thing to do if you don't want to be shouted at.

'You'd better go back to your office and have a long, hard think. Consider your situation and your position here. I need to talk with Shannon about this.'

O'Hara left with his tail between his . . . Damn. Let's not go there.

'What advice do you have for me, Shannon?'

'I think it's best if he falls on his sword.' I gave in on the cliché front. I wondered if Valentine was counting, to entertain the others when we got back. 'It's complicated,' I said. 'We only have his word that he was going to repay what he had taken. He could have been about to skim off anything over a million. He might have intended to put the growth in his own pocket. Can you trust him ever again, is the key question.'

'You know,' he said, 'I was all set to cancel our contract in the light of Bradley's death and how that might have affected the share price. Now I'm not quite so sure. You've only been here five minutes, and you discover a fraud of a couple of hundred grand. I'm left asking myself what else is lurking in the muddy pool. You do make life difficult, Shannon. But that's your reputation and you're living up to it.'

'Have you had time to look at your clients and make an assessment of who might go, fearing for their lives?' I said.

'All the account directors are phoning clients as we speak, to reassure them the killing had nothing to do with us, apart from occurring at the fair.'

'And,' I said, 'what about the imponderables of how it might have knock-on effects when you're pitching for new business? What's your best estimate?'

'How many angels can dance on a pinhead?' he said. 'Reputations can take years to build and five minutes to lose. I'm left wondering if my time here is spent. What's your best guess as to how long it might take you to wrap things up?'

'End of the week should do it,' I said. 'Maybe two weeks depending on what we find. It might be good for your staff to keep on as if nothing has changed. The police are involved now, too. They could have caught the killer by then.'

'End of the week it is, then,' he said.

Back to square one.

* * *

Valentine and I decided to stick to the original plan of interviews set up by Brookie. Next on our list was Mike Wolfe, Creative Director. The ideas king of the agency.

His office was on the director-level fifth floor. Befittingly, it was a large room with windows looking down to the busy streets below. There was a table, probably glass, but I couldn't see the top due to every part being obscured by chaotic paperwork, four chairs and an architects' easel with a drawing of a rabbit on it. There was a cosy sitting area with two sofas and a coffee table with a chess board on the top. That was where Wolfe directed us to sit. It wouldn't be cosy for long.

There was a bookcase behind one of the sofas. The books, mostly on art and artists, were higgledy-piggledy except three books that stood out: *Mein Kampf* by Adolf Hitler; *The Prince* by Machiavelli; *The Art of War* by Sun Tzu. Here was a man that took no prisoners. I guessed that when he stood up he would be short like Napoleon and Hitler.

We sat, expecting a hard time.

He rose from behind his desk. I would have won the bet on his height. He had an overlong, scraggly beard, eyes of an indeterminate colour somewhere between blue, and grey, unruly hair. He was dressed like a fifties beat poet in cord trousers, overlong sweater and suede shoes.

'I'd be grateful,' I said, 'if we could start with some background. Tell me about yourself, Mister Wolfe?'

'How is that relevant?' he said.

Great start.

'I need to get an idea,' I said, 'of the reactions to the share sale. Who will subscribe and who, not being able to afford it, will leave disillusioned. Hence needing some background on the key players, you being one. So, let's start again. Tell me about yourself.'

'There's not much to tell,' he said.

Which in my book meant the exact opposite. There would be interesting detail left out that we would have to eke out of him.

'Father was an engineer and wanted me to follow in his footsteps. He knew I liked art, but that wasn't a proper job. I defied him and went to art college. Did well there, and did graphic design projects on the side to make some money. Went into advertising as a trainee art director and climbed the greasy pole from there. Forty years old, happily married, no mortgage on our house in Islington, and here I am.'

He looked intensely at his watch as if to say he wanted to draw more rabbits.

'So, the creative process,' I said. 'How does that work? What are the steps along the journey to an ad appearing in a newspaper or on TV?'

'The client gives us a brief — a few objectives or targets to reach and what evidence they have, with internal and external data such as focus groups and large-scale surveys. Got that so far?'

I didn't bother answering him: it wasn't a question, but an expression of power.

'Every account has an account planner. It's his job to translate that brief into something we can work on and supply us with all the background — who is the target group; what are the competition doing; how does the consumer talk, so we can address the target group in terms that are relevant to them; what they think about the products in the market and lots more. You should talk with the head of planning, if you didn't have her on your list.'

'The process?' I prompted him again.

'From the brief, we enter the creative phase. Formulate some ideas, work them up into something we are able to show to client. If the client buys what we offer, we go into action. Work up all elements and then pass them through to the production department for the hard, routine phase of getting everything right to pass to the press or TV companies. Oh, before that phase, the media must be selected — planned and bought. We need to know what we are working with. If we're lucky, we get a reward by winning a prize or, simply, have a happy client — which, I suppose is the name of the game.'

'What do you think of the putative share placement? Will you be buying?'

'Depends,' he said.

He wasn't making things easy. Almost as if everything was below him.

'Depends on what?' I asked.

'In essence, I'll be in the market for some. The price would have to be right. Significantly, that means taking the current situation, rather than the one before Bradley's death.'

'Any clients you think might go?' I said.

'The suits — the account directors — will have an idea about that. They'll give you a better picture.'

'How about new business?' I said. 'Will Bradley's death put some of them off?'

'Clients choose an agency because of its ads. Nothing will change there, as long as we keep our standards up. That's why the creative department is the most important part of the business.'

'Any creatives that could be attracted to go — poached — in these unusual times?'

'My people are loyal to me. They'll stay all the time I am here. I'm their Spartacus. If I ever decide to leave, most will come with me.'

'That would be a big hiatus,' I said. 'Having you locked into the agency with shares and with your name on the door would be the smart move all round.'

'I have control now,' he said. 'That would have to continue in the future.'

'And what about the money side of things?'

'Like a said before, pad in Islington. Fully funded.'

'At the moment, you sound cash-rich. How much would you prepared to stake?'

'What it took. Half a million. Perhaps. Whatever the final shareholders and their stakes, I would need control. And on that note, our interview is over.'

* * *

We got back inside our room and found that someone — my bet was on the vigilant Brookie — has provided us with vacuum flasks of tea and coffee, together with all the necessary provisions, including a plate of chocolate digestives. We drank and munched.

'Well, Valentine, what did you make of our friend, Wolfe? And I use the word *friend* loosely.'

'He seemed a little aggressive,' he said.

'Just a little? What about the books on his shelves? Hitler and the like? You did notice them?'

'Obviously,' he said. 'You're training me well, and I couldn't miss the import. He's a control freak. Prepared to learn from anyone, even Hitler, to up his standing to be number one. Will do anything for the welfare of his soldiers.'

'Right,' I said, 'the next appointment is with the media director. Let's use our time wisely. From you, I would like you to look at the HR files and write the name and address of all our key people all on a separate page: include photos from the security passes. Once you've written them out, estimate the travel time and cost of getting to their home and back. When we get back, draw cash from Morag. Forty pounds plus travel costs for today and tomorrow. Meanwhile, I have some tedious work to do on the accounts.'

'What about Bradley?' he asked. 'Do you have any thoughts on his last word?'

'Oh, I know all about that . . . and yet I know nothing about it.'

'Is this a test?' he said. 'Will it be included in my three-month appraisal?'

'It will be part of this afternoon's appraisal, so don't spend too much time on lunch. Do what you youngsters do when they want to know something. Use your phones.'

* * *

I popped downstairs to the restaurant and bought a selection of dim sum and a paper cup of light soy sauce for our lunch. We were quiet, save for the moans of delight created by the dim sum and the whirring of our brains.

Despite this year's accounts looking healthy at first glance, turnover — revenue — had been stable at best over the last two years, after gaining in the two years before that. The trend was down. I asked Valentine to come and look at the figures.

'What do you make of this?' I said, to test his nose.

'Not much difference,' he said. 'Good regular profits. A bit lower lately, but nothing out of the ordinary.'

'Tell me about inflation?' I said.

'Inflation has been high,' he said, puzzled.

'How does an agency make the majority of its revenue?' I said.

'By this magic fifteen per cent cut it takes on media spend.'

'Presumably, media has been subject to inflation, too. Therefore, the agency's take will be larger. Make sense?'

'Theoretically,' he said. 'There must be something strange, otherwise you would not be asking me questions. What about clients cutting back on their spend in these hard times?'

'Could be,' I said. 'It's a rough time for everyone. Advertising is an easy thing to cut back on. It's something we should check with the media director later. I smell a rat somewhere.'

I examined the breakdown of costs on where the spending was going. A couple of items warranted further delving, one being lunches at extravagant restaurants. Maybe that was part and parcel of the advertising industry and it would never stop; maybe it was taken for granted by clients who had watched *Mad Men*.

Much of the overall cost at Pym's was salaries — nothing else could be done away with. All the directors had pricey cars which they couldn't use to get to work due to there being no place to park. I wondered how long that perk would last when it was a future where the enhanced board of directors had shares and the costs came out of their pockets.

The media director's name was Desmond 'Des' Hawkins. He had the warmest handshake I have ever known. It was warm in heat and warm in the grip that he gave me with both hands as he pumped up and down. His office was smaller than Wolfe's, but had a much more homely feel. There were bright modern abstracts on the magnolia walls and three diplomas from organisations in the media world. His desk was neatly arranged and had the usual photo of his family. Compared to those who had it out of habit or requirement and ignored it throughout the day, I could imagine him looking lovingly at it while drinking coffee. I liked him immediately. I hoped he didn't prove me wrong.

He motioned us to the two sofas in the room placed opposite to each other, either side of a coffee table laid out with coffee and tea in vacuum flasks.

'I thought we could make it informal,' he said. 'Let me get you coffee or tea.'

Both Valentine and I went for tea, our coffee limit having been passed already that day. While he poured, I took a closer look at him. He was about fifty, I guessed, but good for his age. He was tall and spare; I put him on some sort of fitness routine to maintain weight and stem the progress of middle-aged spread. The part of him that did look his age was the lack of hair on the top of his head; the two sides had been trimmed carefully, but there was no disguising that soon he would be totally bald. His face was clean-shaven and his brown eyes had a glow to them. He had on a plain light grey suit with a blue shirt, red tie and shiny black brogues. Everything neat and tidy. Palmer would have liked him, too.

'Nice tea,' I said. 'Assam?'

'No,' he said. 'Free. Courtesy of our beverage client. He sends over a batch every month so that we always use his brand. Think what we could do if we had discount on a wine or spirits client.'

'No one would ever be sober.'

'As you say,' he laughed. 'Except Mike Wolfe is teetotal, so won't hear of it.'

Yet his staff smoked weed. Interesting view of the world. Ready to bend the rules when it suited him.

'Where would you like to start?' Des said. 'I've kept the afternoon free, so don't worry about taking too much time.'

'Tell us more about your role in the business?' I said. 'How do you fit in? What does your cog in the machine do?'

'I have two parts in my role here. I oversee media planning — where we should place the ads or commercials according to the target group — and what can we get it for. Each account has a media planner and buyer assigned to it. Those individuals will cover between five and ten clients each depending on how big the budget, and details such as

71

specific events — Christmas being manic. I've arranged for a meeting with a team tomorrow. Brookie has rearranged your schedule.'

'How did you start out?' I said. 'It seems a complex procedure. What caused you to even think about media as a career move?'

'Business studies at Bristol. Loved it. My other choice was modern languages, and I'm so glad I didn't do that, spending all my time on boring translations. Media is so varied and so challenging. Every day is different. I tend to class it as ephemeral — fleeting, short-lived. Think of the newspapers — only last for one day. You have to grasp every opportunity with both hands.'

'How many years have you been here?' I said.

'Three months short of ten years. It's a big happy family here, with the odd black sheep in it.'

'I noticed,' I said, 'that there hasn't been much growth in the last two years. What's your theory on why that is?'

'Mike Wolfe has — how can I put this? — a certain *confrontational* style. Not all clients like that — not all staff, too, to be honest, but he's the creative director, and that's the name of the game.'

I thought we had found our black sheep.

'Confrontational in what way?' I said.

'He has some — and again here I'm searching for words — *unusual* ideas and defends them to the death. Last year, he convinced a client to spend all the year's budget in one day by taking every ad he could in just one newspaper. It caused a stir among agencies — no one had ever done that before — but any effects soon died away, and sales fell each month after that. Another time, it was making a commercial without any branding or client name, his rationale being that it would tease the audience into getting off its sofas and finding out what the product was. It didn't. The client took his business elsewhere.'

'This doesn't square with your comments about Pym's being one big happy family. Sounds like there's a lot of tension below the surface,' I said.

'Creative directors are like football managers. They start with ideas and theories, and the new regime brings results purely from being a change — a fresh face. That's called the Hawthorne Effect — look it up on Wiki. The football club cuts the slack that was initially given. In all, bar the very best managers, the effects dwindle. Success for the club ebbs away. The secret is to know when to cut your losses.'

'Any business has petty rivalries,' I said. 'Are you saying for Pym's, it's more than that?'

'Mike is very protective of his staff,' Des said. 'Some might say too much and that they get away with murder, if that isn't an insensitive phrase to use in the current circumstances.'

'Would you be buying some shares?' I asked.

'I would have to think very carefully about it,' he said. 'In the current regime, no.'

'If Wolfe goes, it sounds like your answer would be yes. Is that right?'

'Mike is a great believer in gestalt theory — the whole is better than the sum of its parts — and the zeitgeist — the very spirit of the times. I have no idea where he is coming from. More tea?'

We nodded. While he poured, we had a pause to think of the import of what he was saying.

'Any questions, Valentine?' I asked. Give the lad his head.

'How do you decide where the ads should go — press and TV, social media and so on?' he said.

'That's the job of the media planner. It depends on the budget — making the most of the client's resources — and the target group. The smaller the target group, the more it costs to reach one member of that audience — in general, that is; there are exceptions. Minimising the cost is where the clever work goes on. Once a strategy has been agreed — that's the job of the account planner — the media buyer steps in and tries to get the best deal possible. I happen to think that we have some of the best media planners and buyers, and account planners, in the industry. We should make more of them, if allowed. The account planners — those whose part of the job is to assess the success of the campaign — are viewed as challengers to his team, traitors even — and are often overridden by the creatives on the grounds, that they don't appreciate the benefits of fresh thinking.'

'And again, Valentine,' I said.

'So how do you work out whether a campaign is successful or not?' he said.

'There are easy ways, one being that a coupon is given away in a press ad and that coupon has a code number on it. From that, we can tell the relative success of different publications. Otherwise, the account planner steps in and commissions some market research — focus groups or quantitative studies. The account planner will explain more when you meet her tomorrow.'

'One last question, Valentine,' I said.

He hesitated.

'The one word,' I prompted.

'Oh, of course. What can you tell me about McLuhan?'

'Marshall McLuhan,' said Des. 'Best known for his phrase "the medium is the message".'

'Can you explain it?' Valentine said.

'I'll give you an example. Suppose you want to place a small ad in a magazine. The ad reads "naughty boy needs strict disciplinarian". If you place that ad in *Tatler* or the *Lady* you get a response from a Norton's Nanny or similar. If you place in a magazine like *Penthouse* or similar, who do you get responding?'

'Ah,' said Valentine. 'I think I understand it now.'

'There's more to it than that,' Des said. 'You should do some bedtime reading.'

'Were you at the fair on Saturday?' I asked. 'Tragic.'

'I was there with my wife,' he said. 'Opportunity to schmooze the clients. More business than pleasure, I'm afraid. There's going to be a lot more schmoozing to do after Bradley's death.'

'What do you remember of the event?' I asked.

'We were making our way back after going clockwise rounds the fields. Heard the screams. Like the sound of the banshee, O'Hara would say.'

'How close were you to the ghost train when you heard the screams?'

'We were at the back of the ghost train,' he said. 'Too close. My wife has had nightmares the last two days.'

'And you didn't see anything suspicious? No one coming out through the canvas at the back of the ghost train?'

Just as we were getting somewhere, his secretary interrupted us. 'Mister Pym wants you in the boardroom,' she said. 'You, too, Mister Shannon.'

We made our way to the boardroom to find everyone assembled, some faces I knew and some yet to be questioned. With one notable exception. O'Hara.

Pym took a long breath. 'I have to inform you that O'Hara has resigned.'

He had done the decent thing and fallen on his sword.

'About time,' said Wolfe. 'He was always questioning me about my expenses. So do we have anyone in mind for a replacement?'

'We'll put feelers out; see if anyone seems restless and up for a challenge. The accounts manager will handle everything on the normal day-to-day running until we find a replacement.'

'How about promoting her?' Des said. 'We need another woman's voice on the board. It would do away with someone new learning about us and how we handle the business.'

'I like the sound of that,' said Wolfe, probably thinking a woman would be easily bullied.

'Let's give it a try,' said Pym. 'Three months' probation. At the end of that, we'll know whether she can handle it or not.'

'Do we know why he resigned?' said Des. 'It's a bit sudden, especially with your share placement coming up.'

'Let's just say,' said Pym, 'that he mismanaged the agency's finances.'

'Caught with his hand in the till,' laughed Wolfe.

'I'm determined,' said Pym hastily, 'that the share placement goes ahead as planned. A delay is good for no one. We need certainty about the future of the business. I am proposing, if he will accept, that we widen Shannon's role to get him to calculate a fair price for the shares. Is that acceptable, Shannon?'

I nodded and looked round the room. The only person frowning was Wolfe. He would be a strong antagonist, opposing me to the end.

'Then it is done,' said Pym. 'I'll email the staff, and I think we could say O'Hara resigned to spend more time with his family. I'll speak to the accounts manager after this meeting. Business done. Let's get down to making money.'

Amen to that.

CHAPTER ELEVEN

Valentine and I headed home on the Tube and the DLR full of more unanswered questions than we had started. It was beginning to become aggravating not having the car for all our luggage — laptops from Pym's as well as our own, various paperwork and the HR files. I suppose I should live with *aggravating* in the current situation. I wondered if Palmer was doing any better than us in solving the murder.

We picked up the Beamer, and made our way to what was now a familiar destination. Arthur's white van was parked up and I guessed he was already into the day's practice session. When we got to the patch of concrete, the fun was going on. Ten youngsters sparring with each other. 'How are they doing?' I said to Arthur.

'Don't stand a cat in hell's chance of disabling a kid with a knife, but they're improving and I'm happy. I'd like to say it keeps them off the streets, but that's exactly where we are.'

'Let's go for a walk,' I said.

The three of us walked towards the ghetto of the tower blocks and saw nothing to boost our spirits. At the bottom of one of the blocks was that small parade of shops — newsagents, tobacconists and confectionary, second-hand furniture, launderette, and two empty premises with notices in the windows saying they were now the property of official receivers. What a place to grow up.

'Are you still shadowing us during the day?' I said to Arthur.

'Of course,' he said. 'Not that I can do much with you travelling by trains, but I've hung around for a while outside your offices and kept an eye on Cherry and Anji today. Boy, can they shop! I've not spotted anything unusual. Nothing to worry about so far.'

'Long may it stay that way,' I said.

'I have an idea,' Valentine said.

'Is it the same as mine?' I said.

'I expect so,' he sighed, 'seeing how you're always one step ahead of me.'

'That's the way to learn,' I said. 'Tell me more.'

'It's the hairdressers, isn't it,' he said. 'Empty premises. Ripe for a change of use.'

'Time to talk with the landlord. Can't do any harm,' I said.

'Why are you doing this?' Arthur said. 'Why are you doing what you're thinking of doing?'

'Someone's got to do something,' I said, 'and I seem to be the only game in town.'

'Is it an honour thing again?' Valentine said.

'When you have honour, no truth can hurt you,' I said.

'Wow!' Valentine said. 'Profound. Although I don't think I know what your words mean.'

'I'm not sure I do, either,' I said, 'but it gives a rationale for making risky decisions.'

I took down the details of the landlord of the premises and we drifted back and interrupted the training session. Arthur got them lined up.

'I have a task for each of you,' I said. 'I want you to keep an eye on some people for a couple of hours in the afternoon and early evening for a few days. I want to know what their house looks like. I want to know what cars they drive, apart from the ones in these files. You've got addresses here and photos of them. I want to look inside their heads. The task pays twenty pounds a session. Valentine will give you the first payment in a moment. He'll also give you money to get to these addresses. He's checked it out, so don't think you can claim more than he's giving you. Let's go.'

'Who rides a bike?' Valentine said.

Four hands went up.

'You get the nearest ones,' he said. 'If anyone asks what you're doing, it's a problem with your bike — chain came off, or something.'

He distributed the four files, then gave out the rest and guidance that if they were approached to say they were out jogging and hurt a muscle. Hoodies were barred. They — my irregulars — were to be non-suspicious and non-threatening. Any trouble, and they were to return here. Training sessions were to be earlier in the day so they could be on surveillance for the necessary hours. Surveillance should be from five in the afternoon, when the suspects were coming home from work, and seven in the evening, when they were likely to be settled down for the night.

I asked Arthur if he would like to join us for dinner when he was finished. He smacked his lips. Valentine and I drove back and found nobody downstairs. We went up to the communal area and our eyes were assaulted. Bearing in mind it was the whole floor, so there was bags of space . . . *bags* was the appropriate word.

There were bags everywhere. On the floor and on the seating. You had to be careful where you walked. 'What's going on?' I asked.

'We've been shopping,' said Anji.

'I can see that,' I said. 'If shopping was to be an Olympic event, you've just won the gold medal.'

'We've been shopping for the wedding,' said Cherry. 'A girl needs lots of things for a wedding. I found a delicious dress. I'd love to show it to you, but it would be bad luck.'

'Is there anything left in the shops?' I said.

'Nothing that's any good,' said Anji. 'Wait to see the jewellery.'

'Jewellery?' I said.

'Of course,' said Cherry. 'You have bought a ring?'

'It's on my to-do list,' I said.

'It's size J,' Cherry said. 'Something gold would be good.'

She had thought of everything. Oh, God, I hoped it would all work out like in her dream. Disappointment was banned.

I walked over to the bar and poured a large vodka with a splash of orange juice. Took orders from everyone as to what they wanted and started work on the drinks. After taking a gulp of mine. Anji and Cherry both went for diet tonic, as part of a two-week crash-diet plan.

'I don't feel like cooking tonight,' Cherry said. 'I thought we could get a Chinese.'

'Have to be a big one,' I said. 'I've asked Arthur to join us.'

'Just a little duck for Anji and me. Nothing fried. I suppose we shouldn't really have the duck, but I have a real fancy for some.'

I cleared a seat on one of the sofas and sat down with the menu. I called the Chinese and ordered a selection of dishes for eight o'clock. That's the only habit I copy from the French: dinner at eight. Such a civilised time.

Cherry and Anji disappeared to their respective rooms and the bags were whisked away. Valentine set the table with chopsticks, plates and bowls, and bottles of light and dark soy sauce. We were all prepared. Arthur joined us, had a beer and we waited. And waited. Evidently there was a lot of trying on to be done.

Palmer arrived at a quarter to eight, and declined a drink and our invitation to join us, claiming that his wife would lynch him if he did. He sat down and looked expectantly at me. 'Any progress?' he asked.

'I found one person committing embezzlement and one who was glad to see him go. Other than that, things seem normal. However, our remit has changed. Not only have we been asked to check that everything at Pym's is honest, but we now have to set a fair price for the shares. It's early days yet, but I have a feeling that something's not right. Whether it's related to Bradley's death, I don't know. Time will tell. As ever. We've not found anything of value from the files on the laptop or the papers from his house. Can't trace the money he was getting, because it's cash. Dead end. What progress from the Seeco side? Any grudges from his colleagues?'

'They're all as white as the driven snow,' Palmer said.

'We know more about the one word he uttered before he died,' I said, 'but nothing that makes any sense. It's a case of "keep shaking the tree and seeing what fruit falls to the ground".'

'None better at shaking the tree than you,' he said. 'But you get more practice.'

'If we're right about Bradley's last word, the answer will be somewhere in the media chain. We're seeing two people tomorrow. Maybe that will help to solve the riddle. His wife said he liked puzzles, and that's certainly what he's created.'

'What's your bet our boffins will find something that you missed on his laptop?' Palmer said.

'I hate to be immodest, but the chances are slim. It's what we do all the time. More practice again. Practice makes perfect.'

Palmer shook my hand. 'Keep me posted. Watch yourself. The stakes must be high to warrant killing Bradley. You might just be next.'

'Who would want to kill me?' I said. 'On second thoughts, I'll watch myself.'

CHAPTER TWELVE

Anji was at a loose end — shopping done, report finished and client invoiced — so I took her along to Pym's while Valentine was assigned to going through all of Bradley's material a second time to make sure we hadn't missed anything. I had a specific task for her, too — opinion on rings, knowledge of which I was extremely lacking. We had a meeting booked for nine thirty, so joined all the other commuters squashed into the carriages of the underground. We had to change lines, so waited on a packed platform for the next train. I marvelled at how the seasoned commuters knew exactly where the train's doors would stop and formed a knot at those points. We were in between them and standing room would be limited and seats impossible. The digital screen said that the next train would be two minutes. I placed my bags on the floor in between my legs and prepared for the scrummage that would occur when the passengers disembarked. I looked straight ahead at a poster for Seeco crisps and wondered how long it had taken Ned to arrange the package over a background yellow. Advertising didn't look hard from this angle.

'Hatton Garden seems the best place to start for the ring,' I said to Anji. 'Let's go there at lunchtime. We could pick up some falafels to eat when we get back. I'll be so much happier when I've got the ring in my pocket. What a relief that will be.'

'Any ideas?' she said.

'Gold, obviously,' I said. 'Diamonds?'

'Maybe too flashy,' she said. 'Let's see if something catches our eye.'

The screen now said one minute. I could feel the air as it was punched down the tunnel by the approach of the train. I saw a light from it now, too.

And then it happened.

I felt a big push in the middle of my back, and I was propelled over the edge of the platform and landed between the rails. The train was only yards away and there was no escape.

I stretched out my arms and lay as flat as I could, pressing my body right down so I could feel the gravel between the tracks on my cheeks.

The train ran over me.

I let out the breath I had been holding.

I heard a voice shout, 'Are you alive?'

'No,' I shouted. 'Get this train off me.'

The train backed up and I had a choice to make. One of the three tracks was live, and I had no idea which! Rather than lying there waiting an indeterminate amount of time for rescue, I raised my body straight up and carefully moved towards the platform edge, touching nothing. You don't realise just how low the tracks are compared with the platform until you look up at it. I raised my arms and felt a reassuring grip on them. Together, two men got me back up to the platform.

'That man pushed you,' a woman shouted.

'What man?' I asked.

'He was here a moment ago,' she said. 'He's disappeared.'

'What did he look like?' I said.

'I only got a glance,' she said. 'Tall man, black raincoat. Dark hair. Just ordinary.'

'Black or white?' I said, trying to dig into the inner regions of her memory.

'White,' she said. 'That's all. It all happened so fast.'

'This confirms my thinking,' I said to Anji.

'Which is?' she said.

'We're on the right track.'

She groaned.

* * *

Anji got coffee. She added sugar and gave it a stir. I tried to lift it to my lips, but my hands were shaking as the adrenaline flushed through my body and quit its duty.

'You know,' she said, 'if you're going to choose an employer, choose a lucky one. If you've got the nine lives of a cat, Nick, you're getting through them very quickly.'

I was dishevelled for our meeting, and there were patches of oil on my jacket and trousers. I reflected what might have happened, and thought that Lady Luck had been on my side. I made a point that I had to play down how serious it could have been when I recounted the story later. I felt an inner voice saying that it was time to quit Pym's, but I would not give up. It was not in my nature. Stubborn to a fault.

The two people welcomed us into their cosy office with its terracotta walls and simple beige carpet, and introduced themselves.

'Emma Potter,' the woman said. 'Media planner. Relieved to be able to do something fun with my stats degree.'

She was petite and was bright and cheery: she looked like someone it would be good to be around. She had long multi-coloured hair with the prominent shade purple. Her eyes were big and sparkling between an oversized pair of glasses. She was wearing what used to be called grunge, and might still well be, for all I knew. Multilayers ending in a long velour skirt and suede ankle boots. It had a feel of gipsy about it. She was around thirty and looked the sort of girl who liked nothing better than sitting in a pub with her friends over a glass of cider.

Her workmate introduced himself as:

'Richard Cawley. Call me Rich, because it's true.' He laughed unself-consciously at his own joke, even though he must have used the words countless times.

He was around twenty-five years old and a couple of inches below average height. His hair was black and eyes were dark brown. There was a large, vivid red birthmark on the right side of his face, a difference from his peers that might have been the cause of bullying him as a kid. I hoped not, for his sake. Nothing worse in life than starting it being demeaned. Though, his tone of voice — East End with the edges rounded only slightly — appeared confident, so maybe I'd reached the wrong conclusion.

He was wearing a suede jacket that I admired and skinny blue denim jeans with slits cut in at his legs over ankle boots. His brilliant white T-shirt made me wonder if he was still living with his parents or, failing that, a fastidious partner. The watch on his wrist shouted luxury from the amount of gold that shone like a beacon. *Flash* was the descriptor that came into my mind. He didn't care what his gainsayers thought of him. Would disregard his detractors and bathe in the scented bath of his followers. I sensed that he was ripe for some other means of making money so that he could flaunt at a higher level. In short? I didn't like him.

'Tell me what you do exactly, and how you fit together?' I said.

'So, I'm the media planner,' said Emma, 'and Rich is the media buyer. The whole process starts with the brand strategy and objectives which the account planner and account director put together. From this comes the target audience, who we're aiming to reach. We're going to use a sniper rifle rather than a shotgun. The next factor to be fed in is the budget. These determine the overall plan, and it's up to me to come up with the detailed plan — which media to use to make the most of the budget. Des is involved in all decisions here. So together, we get to the point of handing over to Rich to see what deals he can get.'

'The wheeler-dealer is me,' he said. 'Though not all the time. Hang there with me, Shannon. There are two ways to do it. Take TV as an example. I can construct an individual made-to-measure deal spot by spot, or I can go for a package. The TV companies have packages they can pick off the shelf that guarantee a certain level of coverage among our target group for a certain budget, and all including at least one high profile spot — in the middle of *Love Island*, say.'

'Which of the alternatives do you tend to go with?' I said.

'A package is simpler,' he said, 'but it takes away from using the best of my tools. There's more challenge for me. More fun. More satisfaction.'

'I saw a poster for Seeco crisps this morning on the Tube. Does the same process apply to that, the same as TV?'

'Whatever the medium is — TV, posters, press, social media,' he said, 'there's an opportunity for an element of negotiation. And that's how I can make the money go further and earn my keep. Next question.'

'May I?' Anji said, looking at me. 'How do you verify what ads or commercials you have booked actually take place?'

Rich turned to her and, hopefully, wouldn't be patronising.

'All ads — all campaigns—' he said, 'come with a schedule showing what day, time, programme slot, so it's easy for the client to verify, if they want to get involved in micro-management, which most don't. We do, though, contract with a company who does exactly that. For other media, say for press, we are sent a voucher copy to make sure everything is OK — the picture has been properly printed, colours correct and in register and so on.'

'Can you get me voucher copies for the last two months?' I said.

'It's going to be a lot,' Rich said.

'We're willing workers,' I said.

'Going back to packages,' Anji said. 'Does that do away with the need for a buyer? Anyone could pick a package. Do you feel threatened at all? The threat of redundancy ever present?'

'As Emma said earlier,' he said, 'we use a sniper rifle rather than a shotgun. We want every bullet to count, not flayed away with shot going everywhere. I get a chance to show my worth by negotiating about what I don't want and what I do. There is always some leeway.'

'And the creatives?' I said. 'What role do they play in the process?'

'A big one,' said Emma. 'Basically, they tell us what they need — the first commercial in the campaign should be sixty seconds, say, rather than the norm of thirty, and needs a mass market viewing in the first break in *Love Island* to kick start the campaign.'

'Do the media offer incentives to get you to book with them?' Anji asked. I liked the way her question was going. *Anyone giving kickbacks?*

Emma laughed. 'I get to go to Manchester to show the client the poster sites we have booked, and Rich goes to a supposedly unmissable media conference in Barbados. Want a seat at the Wimbledon final? A box at Ascot or Epsom? Go to the media, and they will arrange it. Lots of sweeteners — goody bags with expensive watches and the latest bit of tech. Lots of jollies. I don't know how Rich finds time to come into work.'

'Dedication,' he said.

'Can you give us an idea of scale?' I said. 'What sort of money are we talking about for a TV ad?'

'A thirty-second commercial during the daytime is about three or four grand,' Rich said. 'The same ad during *Love Island* is around thirty thousand. If you bear in mind that the number of ads seen needs to be around forty times to solidly get the message across, you can see how quickly it all adds up.'

'So what does it all add up to?' I asked.

'A million might be what you need to get an impact,' Emma said. 'That might be spread over a month. Then you might have to repeat it all two or three times a year. The upshot? Nothing less than a million for one month's burst is worth spending.'

Big money, it seemed. And when there's big money, there would be temptations for big scams.

'It's not all that extreme,' said Emma. 'You can opt for spreading the money across fewer and more important regions. You don't have to go national. It's all these things that affect the overall marketing plan.'

'We'll start winding down in a moment,' I said, 'but in the meantime, I'd like to get your reactions on the fair. Did you both go?'

'I'm reminded of the old joke,' Emma said. '"Apart from that, Mrs Lincoln, how did you enjoy the play?" Destroyed an enormous event which should have been fun. The screams were terrifying. I was in the beer tent getting a Pimm's when I heard them. So shocking, such a wail, I dropped my glass and the Pimm's went over my new suede boots. Ruined them.'

'What did you do then?' I asked.

'Took me a while to move,' she said. 'I walked towards the ghost train where a crowd was building. Couldn't see much except the body lying on the ground and you leaning over it. That one sight told me it was time to go. I walked to the entrance, where I was stopped by a police officer. He took down my particulars and let me pass.'

'And how about you, Rich?' I asked. 'Far away or near?'

'My friend and I were looking at some artisan bread and cheese for an evening snack. Heard the screams. Spine-chilling. We had to find out what it was all about, curiosity getting the better of us.'

'Anything out of order around the ghost train?' I said.

'All the people were surrounding it,' Rich said. 'One of those crowds of people who slow down on a motorway to ogle an accident on the other side of the carriageway. The ones who get some pleasure out of the incident and think of themselves rather than the sadness of the victim.'

'Schadenfreude can be a hard taskmaster,' I said. 'Easy to slip into and difficult to process. Did you see anything of interest? People running in panic? People hiding themselves? That sort of thing?'

'I hate to appear uncooperative,' Rich said, 'but isn't this a police matter?'

'Just think of me as an adjunct to the police. Nice little chat to me rather than a bleak interview in a windowless cell inside the police station. I can help them by narrowing the work to be done — tick boxes, eliminate people from their investigation. There must have been at least five hundred people there — just think of the hundreds of hours needed to interview them. Mammoth help by listening to me. I've done this sort of thing in the past. The arrangement worked. If in trouble, call on Shannon. That's what the police say. Now, where were we?'

'I wasn't anywhere near the ghost train,' Richard said. 'I was south of it.'

'So, you were facing the back of the ghost train. Did you see anyone coming out of that canvas? Someone moving quickly or running?'

'I didn't,' he said, 'but I was concentrating on finding the screams rather than looking for anything suspicious. There was so much going on. Five hundred people stopping in their tracks, then hurrying, like me, in the direction of the screaming. Bloodcurdling.'

'OK,' I said. 'Thanks for your cooperation. One last question. So what is our final question, Anji? What do we always ask?'

'What is the question we should have asked?' she said.

Emma smiled. 'Tell me more about McLuhan,' she said. 'That's the question. You've already seen Des, and he would have told you his anecdote, his party piece, of the strict disciplinarian. If you really want to understand media, spend some time reading McLuhan's predictive texts and books. You'll see there some of today's words that we take for granted — "global village", "hot and cold media" and the like. McLuhan was way ahead of his time. Do your research. Been nice to talk to you. Everybody likes talking about themselves, and us in the world of advertising are no exception. Good luck in your task.'

Rich blatantly looked at his gold watch. We took our cue.

* * *

We sat back in our office and ruminated.

'Would you like to work here?' I asked Anji.

'Strange mixture of people here,' she said. 'I liked Emma — she seems like she might be fun. As for Mister Flash Harry, I wouldn't give him the time of day, let alone work beside him. I don't know. Maybe I'm viewing it from the wrong perspective. I only really know working for you. What other boss gets pushed in front of an ongoing train to start his day?'

'We hear them keep saying that this is one big happy family, but there are all these undercurrents. A creative director who effectively calls the shots, sticking his finger into every pie going until he's ruined it. Someone who protects his staff like a mother hen, even allowing one to smoke weed in the office. And that's just for starters.'

'Des seems like a nice honest guy,' Anji said.

'But will he stay if more power goes to Wolfe? And if Des goes, does Pym's start to slide down slowly? Some clients like Wolfe's renegade style, others don't, and they will drift away. Can Pym's win enough new business to replace the old? While I mull things over, I have a new task for you.'

'And that is?' she said warily.

'Find me a parking space for the Beamer.'

She sighed and started some magic on Facebook.

I called up the profit and loss account and had a second look. Predictions about the future are made from looking at past history. This gives you a warm feeling when the graph is going up, but may give a misleading picture when the changes start to happen. The increased remit we now had wasn't just about honesty and integrity; it was crystal-ball gazing regarding the future of Pym's. The ball was cloudy, and I didn't like it that way.

We'd yet to meet with an account director and an account planner, but I wondered how much that would change my views. If I were looking at it from the point of view of an outside investor, I would say to shake hands and walk out the door. How does the song go? Walk out the door;

you're not welcome anymore. I thought how Pym would feel when I reported back. I decided to find out.

I walked up the stairs to his office and Brookie patched me through. She said she'd organise coffee, and that the next meeting wasn't due for an hour. I had enough time for my dredging to take place. Start at the bottom and see what you catch in the net.

'Thanks for fitting me in, sir,' I said. 'I know that these must be difficult and demanding times.'

'You can drop the "sir", Shannon,' he said. '"Vernon" will be fine. As for your unasked question, the phones haven't stopped ringing all morning.'

'And the outcome?'

'Two clients have notified us that they are reviewing us and are going for competitive pitches from other agencies. We are invited to pitch against them, but we all know a verdict won't be coming in our favour. They're going through the motions, that's all. Lost cause. As for our external investors, I would expect they're getting cool on the deal.'

Brookie brought in some coffee. We were silent for a while.

'What's going on, Shannon?' he said. 'I feel the business is starting to crumble before my eyes. What are we doing wrong?'

'I'll finish my interviews tomorrow, and then I hope to step back from the trees and see the wood, or vice versa — I can never remember which way round it goes. I'll have spoken to representatives of all the departments by then and have an overview of the picture for the jigsaw. The outcome depends on the number of pieces.'

He pinged the elastic band on his wrist and drummed his fingers on the desktop. He was getting edgy.

'How committed are you to the share sale?' I said.

'It still seems to be the viable option for me. The days of benevolent dictators have passed. Time for me to hang up my guns and retire gracefully, as Clint Eastwood would say.'

'Who would replace you?' I said. 'Internal? Recruit from outside?'

'We need to up revenue after what will be a catastrophic loss of clients. Bring someone new in who'll bring some business with them. I'd like a woman. Even with the promotion of the accounts manager, we're short of female input.'

'How would your current directors feel about that?' I said. 'Anyone who covets the job?'

'Only Wolfe,' he said. 'I'm beginning to think I made a mistake with him. He virtually runs the show as it is. Power corrupts, isn't that what they say? If I were to let him go — I'll say it — if I sack him, what business will go with him? Cleft stick. If he stays, we lose more of those clients who don't like his authoritarian style. Doom and gloom, whichever way you look at it.'

'I assume you realise that the share price is going downward. That would suit the buyers, but is there anyone else who would benefit?'

'Not that I can think of,' Pym said.

'Someone is trying to stop the sale, or at least end my involvement. There's something I'm missing at the moment. I got pushed in front of a train this morning. If the situation wasn't bad enough with Bradley's murder, it's got worse with an attempt on my life. We're into something very serious here. Any ideas?'

He shook his head. 'We're just an ad agency. We don't threaten anyone. What's the big deal?'

'It could be simply that one of the prospective buyers is trying to depress the price of your shares, but that seems too convenient and too drastic a measure. You don't kill for that kind of money. There's something big going down. I aim to find out what.'

'Good luck. Although you seem to have luck on your side already.'

'Out of interest, where were you when the screaming started?' I said.

'By the spinning teacups. Grandson wanted a ride. It was a good job he was distracted to notice or hear of anything. I hate to think of how Bradley's son will cope. Probably have mental scars throughout his life.'

'So you didn't hear or see anything?' I asked.

'Too busy taking photos,' he said. 'You know what it's like being a grandparent.'

'Not out of any experience,' I said, 'but I can empathise. I don't see me becoming a parent, let alone a grandfather. Anyway, Vernon, we must let you get on firefighting. Obviously keep me posted on the client situation. It might be useful to have a list of clients who will go, who will stay and who are undecided. I'll have to use that to help decide the share price.'

My phone rang as I was walking downstairs. It was Palmer.

'I thought you were supposed to keep me posted. I shouldn't have to listen to the news to get the story of the train incident.'

'Apologies,' I said. 'Things have been a bit hectic this morning. In the news, you say?'

'"Miraculous escape" was the phrase they used on Capital Radio. Anything you'd like to add?'

'We now know that Bradley's death was connected to Pym's. Pym's is the only link between us. Give me time, Palmer, and I might give you a murderer. Everyone I've interviewed so far has an alibi for the time of the murder.'

'The boffins haven't uncovered anything useful from Bradley's papers and laptop.'

'I've got Valentine going through everything a second time, but haven't heard anything from him so far. Do we both have the same feeling?'

'Something big is going down,' he said. 'Murder sounds like organised crime — drugs, prostitution, illegal immigrants, money laundering, that sort of thing. Which one? Who knows.'

'Certainly not me,' I said.

And he cut the connection.

* * *

I called Valentine and asked him to make up another bunch of cash to cover Buzz and crew's money for the second day — we'd debrief them all tomorrow when we would have completed our fact-finding mission among the key staff of Pym's. He'd said that he hadn't found anything new in the Pym's accounts, but he would keep trying. He sounded despondent, and I made a mental note to remotivate him.

Meanwhile, Anji jumped with joy. 'I've got it!' she shouted.

'You've solved the murder?' I said.

'No,' she said. 'I've got you a parking space. It's in a quiet mews about ten minutes' walk away. The owner has gone on holiday and the garage will be available till Friday next week. You could drop me off here with all the luggage and then go and park.'

'Brilliant,' I said. 'We can recce it at lunchtime.'

'Along with the rings,' she said. 'You haven't forgotten about the rings, have you?'

'Top of my list,' I said, 'there being not much else happening.'

'Do I detect a hint of sarcasm in your voice?'

'Let's go now,' I said. 'Grab the bull by both horns. Get it ticked off my list of things to do.'

We walked downstairs, still not trusting the rickety lift, and into what little sunlight managed to find its way through the high and narrow streets of Soho. We hailed a black cab and alighted at Hatton Garden. We cruised outside the windows of the many jewellers and diamond merchants in the street until Anji said, 'That's the one!'

'I thought you said diamonds could be too flashy,' I said.

'Not this one,' she said. 'It's so subtle. Plain gold ring with inset of one big diamond flanked by two smaller one. See how the diamonds catch the light? We've got to have it. Cherry will be so thrilled. C'mon, c'mon. It's so perfect. Don't waste time, in case someone else buys it.'

Full of nervous energy, she took hold of my arm and pulled me through the double doors. A smartly dressed man in a three-piece suit smiled at us as we entered. There might have been a slight hesitation when he saw the difference in age between Anji and me, but he covered it well.

'We want one of the rings in the window,' Anji said. 'I'll show you which one.' She led him outside and I could see her point at the window. They came back inside and the salesman unlocked the glass and took out a small tray with the ring we wanted, along with others of a similar style. 'Would madam like to try it on?' he said to Anji.

'Oh, it's not for me,' she said, 'I'm just helping to choose.'

'Do you know the size of finger of the lady it will be for?'

'It's size J,' I said, getting into the conversation for the first time.

'This one is too big, but I can have one made for you in that size. It will take a week. I hope that will be right with you.'

It was cutting it a bit fine, but there was no option for the special ring.

'Go ahead,' I said. 'I'll also want a plain gold band for myself.'

The salesman took a tray from under the glass shelf of the desk. It had about fifteen gold rings on it. One stood out immediately. It was a three bears solution — not too big, not too small.

'That's the one,' I said.

'Good choice,' Anji said. 'What a fun day this is becoming.'

'I hate to remind you of me being pushed under a train.'

'Oh, that was hours ago,' she said. 'This is a whole new day.'

* * *

We bought some falafels and took a taxi back to Pym's. While munching, we planned the afternoon. It was now time to meet the recently promoted financial director. After that, we would only need to interview the head of planning, the main-board account director and a second creative team in case we had got the wrong impression with Tony and Ned. Tomorrow should do.

The accounts manager, now financial director, was called Fiona McCloud. When we made introductions, she had spoken with a refined Edinburgh trill similar to the educated tone of Morag.

'Didn't I meet you at the fair?' I said.

'I don't think so,' she said.

'But you were there?'

'Yes,' she said. 'Husband wasn't fussed about going, so I took the dog along for some leisurely exercise.'

'Wasn't it awful?' I said. 'Were you close to it?'

'I heard the screams,' she said. 'I was just coming back from my first round of the fields. They stopped me in my tracks.'

'You must have been close,' I said.

'Not really,' she said. 'The noise was loud and high pitched. I imagine most people must have heard it wherever they were.'

'The ghost train created a big crowd,' I said. 'People milling around the perimeter of it. What do you remember? Were you caught up in the melee?'

'Is this going anywhere, Shannon?' she said. 'We seem to have strayed a long way from the subject of finance.'

'Sorry,' I said. 'Didn't mean to. It was just so traumatic that I can't get it out on my mind. I cradled Bradley as he died.' I shuddered for dramatic effect. 'Let's start again.'

We, finally, so as not to cause any distraction while I was shaking the tree, took seats opposite her at the desk. She looked about fifty and was what might be described as chunky, with a large round face and cheek pouches like a hamster. Her brown hair had been cut too short and was spikey as a result. She was wearing a light blue blouse with an open neck, with a gold chain as the only adornment. She looked ordinary and professional. I guessed she would be wearing a dark skirt and sensible shoes. *Sensible* seemed to sum her up. She was a safe pair of hands.

'Congratulations on your promotion,' I said. 'You must be thrilled.'

'Thank you,' she said. 'I thought it would never happen. I've been here ten years and, I must admit, I had given up hope. College rather than uni probably didn't help.'

'How much did you know about what O'Hara had done?'

'I knew he had taken the money and had invested it. Whenever I raised a question about it, he would shrug and tell me to trust him. Who was I to raise the issue with? Every month, he would tell me to keep the money allocated to the suspense account. I thought O'Hara knew what he was doing and that I shouldn't question his actions. I was worried that I might be seen as disloyal.'

'How do you feel about the share sale? Would you buy some?'

'Probably not,' she said. She was twisting her wedding ring around as she spoke. Displacement activity? 'Out of my league. We're not strapped for cash, but don't have all that much in savings. Shame.'

'Are you nervous about joining the board?' I asked.

'Of course,' she said. 'I might know all the people, but wonder how they act in a formal board meeting. Would I let myself down?'

'Anybody in particular who might make you nervous?'

'I think you know the answer. Wolfe wields so much power that it must be dangerous to go against him.'

'Finally, finances,' I said. 'Do you think things are stable, growing or decreasing?'

'This interview is confidential, isn't it?' she said.

'I won't report back anything you don't want,' I said. 'No notes needed here, Anji.'

'Well,' Fiona said. 'A lot depends on the aftershock reaction to Bradley's murder. What will be the outcome when clients take it all in? Would you, as a client, want to take the risk of something horrific happening again? I don't think so. "Stable at best" is my prognosis.'

'How confident do you feel replacing O'Hara?' I said.

'I can certainly do all the accounting aspects. It's the participation in future planning that worries me. Having been in my job for ten years, I know the place better than anyone. If Pym brought someone in, they'd be a drawn-out learning curve, and can we afford that with the mechanics of the share sale going through?'

'I've looked at the accounts for last year,' I said. 'They've been signed off by the auditors, so I suppose they were happy with them. Were there any questions they asked? Anything they were not sure about? Any clarification needed?'

'Work in progress is always a problem,' she said.

'Easiest way of adding to turnover and, therefore, profits,' I said. 'Or vice versa.' I turned to Anji. 'Work in progress is the unfinished work you've done, but hasn't been invoiced yet. Always a grey area.' I turned back to focus on Fiona. 'Anything else?'

'No,' she said. 'Clean as a whistle, they said. Otherwise, I suppose, they wouldn't have signed them off. They did make a couple of comments about how high people's salaries were, but accepted that that was the way of advertising. When accountants or lawyers start making comments about salaries, then you know they must be high.'

'You're a new broom now,' I said. 'Any changes you'd like to make?'

'All in good time,' she said. 'I need a honeymoon period to settle in. We'll need someone to replace me, and that has to be a priority. I hate to sound unfriendly, but I really need to get some work done.'

'Thanks,' I said. 'Maybe we can come back if we need more answers on specific issues. I must say, though, that from what we've seen of the accounts, you run a tight ship. We're happy with them. If we don't meet again, good luck in your new role.'

We left her smiling.

We went back down a floor and into our temporary office. Moments later, the door was opened by a neat shoe. Brookie came in with a stack of papers a foot high. 'The voucher copies you asked for,' she said. 'I bet you weren't expecting this many.' She laughed.

'Wow,' I said, 'And this is only two months?'

'As you asked for. Don't worry how long it takes — nobody ever looks at them much. Too tedious.'

'How is Mister Pym taking it all?' I said.

'Dear Mister Pym. He's been locked away for much of the day so far talking to clients. I've had to turn a blind eye a couple of times.'

'About what?' Anji said, out of curiosity, after looking at me and waiting for my nod.

'I don't think I will be breaking any confidences,' Brookie said, 'and you must know — everybody knows — that he is a secret drinker. It's worth noting that he is most dependent when he is stressed.'

'But he's trying to break it, isn't he?' Anji said. 'Nick, I mean Mister Shannon, saw the elastic band on his wrist.'

'He goes to AA — I make sure of that. I take him and then bring him back home. I don't think his wife is too happy about the arrangement, but he wouldn't go without my cajoling. There are times when he is really low, when I go in with him and give him encouragement.'

'You must be very devoted to him,' I said.

'Fifteen years, I've been looking after him. I feed him gossip from the staff and he loves it. Keeps his feet on the ground, he says. Anyway, I mustn't leave him alone too long. You understand? Should I send in some coffee or tea?'

'That would be kind. Tea for me,' I said.

'Me, too,' said Anji.

'What are we going to do about all this paperwork?' Anji asked.

'We certainly can't carry it back,' I said. 'We'll go through some now and leave the rest till tomorrow. It doesn't look like the kind of stuff that needs urgent attention.'

We sat and looked at it despondently until the tea arrived. Even then, we took a diversion to talk about Fiona.

'What did you make of her?' I asked.

'A bit mousey,' she said. 'Wolfe will tear her to pieces. She doesn't have the sort of personality to stand up for him. Too introverted?'

'But how long will Wolfe stay for, if his emperor's new clothes are seen for what they are?'

We sipped our tea and looked again at the pile. Time to get our shoulder to the wheel and get our hands dirty. Nose to the grindstone and all those metaphors. Not all of what we do is glamorous or exciting. Shame.

'I'll take the bottom half and you take the top,' I said.

'What are we looking for?' she said.

'Good question.'

She was thoughtful, running her tongue over her lips.

'We're going to shake the tree?' she said.

'Even better question,' I said. 'Let's do it.'

* * *

We worked on till six thirty to avoid the worst of the rush hour, and arrived back home an hour later, due to problems somewhere on some line or other. I wouldn't want to do this every day: the problems indeterminant and daily. It was only the excuse that varied. The first thing I did on our arrival was pick up the vodka bottle. I thought of Pym and put it back down again.

We all gathered in the river room and let the slow passing of the Thames help us to relax. Anji and I debriefed on our day and gave our suppositions on the latest interviews we had conducted. Finally, I had to admit that we were getting nowhere.

'I don't like Wolfe,' I said.

'Me neither,' said Anji. 'I find him creepy. Like he's using some occult power to dominate you. And the books on his shelf. Dictators all.'

'If I were Pym,' I said, 'I would admit I made a mistake and sack him before he does more damage. If the share sale were to go ahead, Wolfe would buy some, and then Pym's is stuck with him. Doesn't bear thinking about. One of the interviews scheduled for tomorrow is with another creative team. I'd like you, Cherry, to come along and give me your unbiased opinion.'

'No problem,' she said. 'I'm virtually finished all the preparations for the wedding. What suit are you going to wear?'

'I hadn't really thought about it,' I said. 'How about the grey one with faint blue pinstripe? Pair it with the blue-and-white striped shirt with the white collar?'

'Um,' she said. 'How about you treat yourself to a new suit. New shirt, too. Factor in a shopping trip tomorrow while I mind the fort. Good idea?'

I nodded and went again to the vodka bottle. Poured a small one and drowned it with some orange juice. I sipped and sighed. 'No problem. Good plan.'

'What do we say, Anji?'

'Tomorrow is another day,' she said.

'Exactly,' I said. 'Roll on tomorrow.'

CHAPTER THIRTEEN

I dropped off Cherry and Anji and drove to the garage. It was a tight fit, and I had to be careful not to hit the driver's door on the wall when I got out, but anything was better than the Tube journey. The walk back also gave me time to produce a mental task plan for the day. We weren't scheduled to meet Pym, but I wanted to call on him to see whether there was anything I could do to improve his mood and keep him away from the whisky bottle. We also factored in that we should allow time in the late afternoon to see if Buzz and gang had found anything useful from their surveillance.

The two people inside the room as we entered were more smiley than I had expected from the duel with Tony and Ned. I warmed to them.

However, we learnt nothing new about the murder and Pym's. We called it a day with them. They weren't killers or fraudsters. I had a nose for both. My mind went back to our interview with the media buyer. I was sniffing there.

'How have you been getting on?' I asked Anji.

'I've created a spreadsheet of gains and losses of clients: by date and by revenue.'

'And?' I said.

'Pretty static,' she said. 'Or, should I say, no overall progress. This isn't a thriving business. It's just jogging along. Hard to predict the future.'

'Which we're going to have to do,' said Cherry.

'The last two interviews to do,' I said. 'Let's be upbeat. Something may well turn up.'

'And how much do you believe that?' said Cherry.

'Not a lot,' I said. 'Anji, go through everything a second time just in case we've missed anything. Onward and upward.'

Cherry and I climbed the stairs and went into the office of Paul Adams, main-board account director. The walls were white and he was sitting behind a glass-topped table as a desk. The chairs were black and gave an austere feeling to the room. Meant to be minimalist, but finished up cold. There were the usual two sofas — black, again — and a coffee table for more informal chats. It was here where Adams directed us. When he'd stood up to greet us, I could see he was average height and thin behind a three-piece suit of black — what else? — with a fat pinstripe of cream. It was a little garish for my liking, but gave the impression of someone who cared for appearances, but was prepared for any judgement. A pocket watch in the waistcoat said it all.

The most remarkable feature of him was a sharp Roman nose. His dark hair was cut in the fashionable Peaky Blinders style of short back and sides and I wondered if he was a trend follower or setter. I put his age as mid-forties, and he didn't look bad for that.

'I've heard a lot about you, Shannon, from my colleagues,' he said. 'The verdict is that you don't care if you ruffle a few feathers.'

'Par for the course,' Cherry said.

'They also say that you seem to be curious about the murder. Correct?'

'Can't deny it,' I said.

'Then shall we start there?' he said. 'At the time of the murder, I was in the beer tent buying Pimm's for a client and

her husband. They can vouch for me. I heard the screams —
spine-tingling — but saw nothing. Now can we start on the
matter in hand, the share sale?'

'In a moment,' I said. 'First tell us how you fit into the
agency.'

'I have my own clients, and I'm responsible for the
account directors below me. Those account directors head
up the team for a client. I'm sure you've learned that already.'

'Head up the team,' I said. 'In theory or in practice?'

'We'll come to that in a moment,' he said. 'So, share sale.'

'How do you feel about it?' I said. 'Opportunity or threat?'

'I would say that now doesn't seem to be opportune for
Vernon. We have no idea how business will be affected by
Bradley's death. Might as well lick a finger and stick it in the
air.'

'If it did go ahead,' Cherry said, 'would you buy some?'

'Too risky,' he said. 'My advice would be to wait six
months and then reappraise the situation.'

'I get the impression Mister Wolfe is quite confrontational.'

'Quite!' he said. 'The understatement of the year.'

'So what should be done about him?' Cherry asked.
'Grin and bear it?'

'Is everything I say off the record?' Adams said.

'Completely,' I said. 'So what's the answer?'

'We have to eat humble pie and admit we made a mistake. Wolfe isn't working. Our client loss equals our new
wins from pitches. You can't stand still. If you do, the mood
in the industry goes against you. This, obviously, affects the
number of invitations to pitch. Potential clients get wary and
you're in a vicious cycle. Time to do the deed, lick our wounds
and hope to find a better replacement this time around. If
we're not careful, staff will get edgy and start looking for a
new job. Overall? Not a pretty picture.'

Time to test the loyalty factor.

'How long have you been here?' I asked.

'Five years. Two years on the board. So, yes, I was on the
team responsible for hiring Wolfe. Have to hold my hand up.'

'Got a family?' I asked.

'Is that relevant?' he said.

'Being a family man often puts pressure on someone,' I said. 'Makes for a lower threshold on risks. Sometimes you don't want to go from pan to fire. Big responsibility.'

'Yes, I'm a family man; wife and two sons. No, I'm not in any financially vulnerable position. I've got the funds to buy shares, and I would have the support of my wife to do so. I don't think there is much else I can tell you. You've got my drift, haven't you?'

'Absolutely,' I said. 'Thanks for your time.'

We went down to our office and took a breather before our final interview.

'We seem to be getting the same story from everyone,' Cherry said. 'Was that your impression from the first batch of interviews?'

'Anji,' I said. 'Tell the nice lady.'

'There's some good people and some horrid ones. Do they make a team? I don't think so.'

'I have a feeling that Paul Adams was right,' I said. 'Hiring Wolfe has been a disaster. He's not going to change his ways. Admit defeat and sack him. Otherwise, it's a slow ride downhill.'

Brookie interrupted us bearing a flask of coffee and all the trimmings. She had to be a mind reader. What a treasure Pym had. He'd be lost without her.

'How has Vernon been doing today?' I asked.

'Dealing with more clients being edgy. The sooner Bradley's murderer is found the better. I'm worried that he's hitting the whisky bottle too frequently. He shouldn't be talking to clients if that's the case.'

'We'll pop in to see him later,' I said. 'The sight of Cherry and Anji might cheer him up.'

'Would you?' Brookie said. 'That would be very kind.'

She left and we sat there sipping our coffees.

'I can't see any way the share sale can go ahead,' Cherry said. 'He'd be selling when the market is at a low. Would his outside institutional investors still be interested? If they did their due diligence, they'd come to the same conclusion as us. Best to restructure, put their house in order and then reintroduce the share sale.'

'In its current state,' I said, 'I would find it hard to pick any more than a multiple of five.'

The multiple is the basis of putting a value on a company. It's a number that you multiply by the post-tax profits, which gives you the company's value. The more sound a company, the higher the multiple and, therefore, the higher the worth. Yes, you have to take any assets — offices and properties — into account, but it's the multiple that's the key figure.

'I wonder how Palmer is getting on,' I said. 'I'll give him a call and see if he can drop in on us. Maybe with his stimulus, we can come up with a solution to the murder.'

We refilled our coffee cups, and I called him. His phone went straight to voicemail, so I left a message. Unusual. He generally took a call from me, as it might be important.

Anji had been working hard, so we decided the three of us would go to the interview with Harry Barker, head of planning. It would be a risk that he would be overwhelmed by so much beauty in one go. And me.

His office was large, but with just the one window. He welcomed us with a damp handshake and I resisted the urge to wipe my hand on my trousers. He was very tall — six foot five, I guessed, the same as Arthur but he was very thin. I sensed from how he dressed — light trousers, loose green woollen sweater, khaki shirt — that he had sprayed himself with glue and walked through a wardrobe.

He was wearing a pair of glasses with such a magnification that it made his eyes seem huge. His hair was mousey and already receding. His desk was littered with paper. There were reams of the stuff in clear folders scattered across the top and several newspapers open at crosswords or sudoku. I sensed the interview would be difficult and contain nothing bar numbers or anagrams.

I let Cherry start. I guessed he might be momma's boy, and that the light feminine touch might work better.

'Harry,' she said. 'May I call you Harry?' He nodded. 'We're concerned how Bradley's murder may have affected staff, especially about PTSD. How are you feeling? You were there, I presume, and may have been shaken by anything that you saw or heard.'

'I'd taken some time out from the socialising with clients and was sitting on one of the benches by the bouncy castle. I was halfway through a cucumber sandwich I had brought with me. I sat up suddenly when I heard the screams. They were so loud, but then I was pretty close to ghost train, and then a dog started barking and the whole place was pandemonium. I saw Shannon kneeling by the body. There was blood everywhere, more blood than you could conceive the body holds. Ghastly.'

'Did you see or hear anything unusual?' Cherry said.

He looked at her with his large eyes as if he couldn't believe what she was saying. 'The whole thing was unusual.'

'Sorry, bad phrasing,' she said. 'Did you see anyone come out of the ghost train?'

'No, but I wasn't really looking at that. My whole attention was drawn to the body at the front. I must admit, I had to turn away. My stomach was doing somersaults and I felt like I might be sick. I didn't want to disgrace myself in front of all those people. I saw nothing but the body with Shannon bending over it.'

'OK, then,' I said, 'let's move on to today's subject. What exactly do you do, Harry?'

'As head of planning, I look after the all the account planners. Every team has a planner attached to it, with similar powers to the account directors. In my humble opinion, the planner is the most important member of the team.'

'In what way?' I asked.

'The planner is the custodian of the consumer or buyer. It's the planner's job to empathise with the consumer. He or she must know everything from the language used through to setting the strategy and, at the end, find out how the advertising performed.'

'So how do the creatives fit into this?' Cherry said.

'The most sensitive regard us as foes rather than friends. After all, we form the strategy and objectives that need to be followed, and are the judges of their work in the final analysis. The rest see us as catalysts to direct their communications with their target group.'

'What background do you need to do the job well?' Cherry said.

'Most important is the ability to have an open mind. Without that, you can't be effective. Then you need to be numerate — my background is a stats degree — and also have an ability to be literate and able to pick up the final points of language.'

'Hence the crosswords and sudoku on your desk,' I said.

'You don't miss much, do you, Shannon?'

'I like to think not,' I said. 'Now the big question. Are you in the market for any of the shares?'

'No,' he said. 'I'm not a risk taker. I could afford it, but I prefer my money safe in the bank.'

'How do you get on with Mike Wolfe?' I said. 'Any tensions there? Any alpha-male struggles going on?'

'He's protective of those who are supportive, and ruthless to those who aren't. It's fair to say we clash from time to time.'

'And who wins?' Cherry said.

'Vernon has the casting vote,' he said.

'And who does he go along with?' Cherry said.

'Wolfe,' he said. 'Vernon gives him his head. Too much slack, in my opinion. He'd do better to rein him in at times. To get him to see the other side of the argument, but I suppose that is part and parcel of creatives everywhere.'

'What would happen, do you think, to your position in the hierarchy of the agency if you don't buy any shares? Would you still be a member of the board?' I said. 'Would you have less power, maybe being outvoted on key issues?'

'Pym's isn't the only game in town,' he said. 'I know I can be seen as a bit nerdy, but I'm good at what I do. I wouldn't have any problem in getting a job elsewhere.'

'Nice position to be in,' I said. 'Always good to have a plan B.'

'But all that may be irrelevant,' he said. 'The share sale won't get off the ground under current circumstances. Too many variables; too many unknowns. The odds are against it.'

'Thanks for your time,' I said. 'It's been very informative. We'll let you get on.'

Back to the office we went. Time for lunch and then a check on Pym. Dim sum again, but who would grumble at that?

Brookie was holding the fort in her area outside Pym's office, screening out those who could come back at a more opportune time. She saw us and nodded us through with an arched eyebrow that Roger Moore would have been proud of. We weren't expecting to find him in the best of moods, but he looked desolate as he sat back in his chair staring at the ceiling. There was a mug containing something, probably diluted alcohol in some form, in front of him.

I introduced Cherry, and the three of us took chairs opposite him in the desk. He smiled at the sight of Cherry and Anji. 'A breath of fresh air,' he said.

'How is it going, Vernon?' I said, dreading the answer.

'The situation can still be saved,' he said. 'I'm surprised just how much loyalty there is among our old clients. After all, it's not often one makes the front page of *Campaign*. The outcome of Bradley's death will be the judge of whether we can carry on in our traditional manner. If it turns out that the murderer is one of our staff, that could well be the end of us as we know it.'

'I've yet to find anyone that I've spoken to that has the classic motive, means and opportunity,' I said. 'We're still digging, but I reserve judgement.'

'It's not going to work, is it?' he said. 'I'm going to have to change my plans, aren't I?'

'"Postpone" would be our recommendation,' I said. 'But let's see what our conclusions will be when we consider everything over the next week. Let's not be defeatist at this stage. I have a good feeling about this.'

It was a lie and, I suspected, everyone knew it, but it was one of those times when the truth could be delayed.

Cherry stretched across the desk and placed a hand on his.

'And how are you coping?' she said. 'It would be easy to sag under all this weight.'

'I thought I had everything under control before this,' he said. 'I was doing well not having a drink, but it's all gone back to where it was before AA. I had it all planned out, and now it's crumpled around me.'

'Look at it as an opportunity to regroup,' I said. 'You've got some difficult decisions coming up — I think you know that. Things aren't working out as they should. Time to reassess your direction of travel. Give it six months and then do your share sale. There's too many imponderables as they are.'

'I'm going to have to get rid of Wolfe, aren't I?' he said. 'Something I should have done a while back.'

'Wolfe is holding you back,' I said. 'His style is too confrontational. Clients will keep drifting away and new opportunities to pitch will dry up. I'll support you — sit in when you have to give him the bad news.'

'I'm grateful,' he said. 'Wolfe can be a bully. I don't know if I can defeat him on my own.'

'It won't be a problem,' I said. 'You can count on me. Lean on me. You better tell the other board members what you are planning to do. I suspect there will be sighs of relief. They'll support you, too. Meanwhile, I'll keep working my way through your accounts. Somewhere there has to be a link to Bradley's murder. I'll come back tomorrow and we can deal with Wolfe. Stay a little while, guys. I'll go and get the car. Bring the last two weeks of vouchers, so we can have a second look at our leisure.'

I left with Cherry still touching the shaking hand of Pym. Anji had a tear in her eye. We would always support the underdog.

I walked down the stairs and into the road. I was five minutes away from garage when my phone went. It was Arthur.

'Don't look back,' he said. 'I'm on your tail. I've got a suspicious man who could be following you. Keep walking and I'll be ready if anything happens. Act natural.'

It's hard to be natural when asked to do so. Your instinct drops away and you start to do the opposite of natural. Think of those times when you are at the doctor's and he says to breathe normally. You can't do it.

I walked on as best I could and reached the garage. I opened the boot and placed my hand inside. Looking up, I saw a heavily built man approach. He had a machete in his hand. Behind him, Arthur was about twenty yards away, the man unaware of his presence. There was no time to wrap my jacket around my left forearm. I picked up the tyre iron from the boot and turned to face him. He hesitated, not thinking there would be any resistance.

He waved the machete and ran towards me. It was how I expected — watch the eyes. It was easy to sidestep as he stumbled past me. I swung the tyre iron and cracked him on his hand. When he had his back to me, I hit him on the shoulder blade. Followed up with another hit on his hand and he dropped the machete. I hit him in the ribcage and he doubled over. He turned, looked up and Arthur joined the fray.

'Well, what have we here?' he said. 'Tyre iron, please, Nick.'

I handed it to him. He took hold of the man and banged him hard against the wall. He forced the man's hand to spread out and hit him on the hand with the iron. The was a sickening crunch. He repeated the process on the man's other hand. Crunch again.

'Right, my friend,' Arthur said. 'Time to talk. Who sent you?'

'I don't know his name, but I have his number. It was just something I heard in a pub. There's a price on your head. Twenty grand to take you out.'

'Dead or alive?' I said.

'Yes,' he said. 'Dead or alive. The price doubles for dead.'

We called 999 and then Palmer — not answering again. We didn't call an ambulance. Bad form, I know, but it was the only way to teach the enemy a lesson and deter other bounty hunters. We told the police it was an attempted mugging and the injuries the attacker had suffered occurred were when he had fallen. As a story, it was about as lame as "slipped on a bar of soap in the shower." I didn't think the police believed us, but they didn't want to get into more paperwork. The attacker went along with it, as he was probably afraid that we would track him down otherwise.

Finally, I was able to drive to Pym's and pick up Cherry and Anji.

'What kept you?' Cherry asked.

'I had an argument with a machete.'

'Which you won,' Cherry said.

'Never in any doubt,' I said.

'So Arthur was there, then,' Cherry said.

'Spoilsport,' I said. 'Another lesson for you, Anji. Don't ruin a good story by telling the truth.'

CHAPTER FOURTEEN

I dropped off Cherry and Anji and picked up Valentine for the debrief of our Baker Street Irregulars. I didn't expect too much new information about our Pym's suspects, but you have to follow up any potential lead. You need thoroughness in a job like ours. Can make for boredom, though, and there is a need to make sure you don't lose concentration.

The dozen or so members of the gang had been marshalled by Arthur and they were all clutching the files we had given them and looking surprisingly professional.

'OK, everyone,' I said. 'Who's got anything interesting?'

Several hands shot up. I called one of them up closer to me.

'What's interesting?' I said. 'Who is interesting and why?'

Here he consulted his notes.

'Richard Cawley,' he said. 'Lives in a flat in Romford. Nothing special. From its reg number, he drives an old car.'

'What exactly is interesting in that?' I asked.

'He changed from his work car and into a different one. It's—' here he consulted his notes again — 'a Lotus Elite convertible. Bright yellow. Looks shiny and as good as new. Wow! What a car. He took it for a spin to show it off. Back in twenty minutes. Settled down for the evening.'

I nodded at Valentine to check it out. He took out his phone and started searching. He was adept at his typing, and soon reported back 'Not much change out of twenty grand for a second-hand one. Much more, if recent.'

'As you say, interesting,' I said. 'Who is next?'

A girl came up to me. 'Tony Lancaster,' she said. 'Like Cawley, he drives a vintage car. Open-top MGB. Stunner. These guys don't know their luck. I'd kill for something like that.'

I frowned.

'Perhaps not kill,' she said. 'I'd die for one, OK?'

And so it continued.

Des Hawkins lived in a detached house in Shoreditch. Expensive, but what you might expect from a director of an ad agency.

Ned Cork lived in a flat in Battersea and drove a red, white and blue Mini that was in the file.

Paul Adams, account director, lived in the suburbs west of London in a detached house that backed on to a golf course.

Harry Barker, head of planning, took the train to and from work. Lived in a small flat in Chingford.

Nobody else looked too extravagant or ostentatious with their money. Well, it was worth a shot.

I moved to Buzz and put one hand on his shoulder. 'Time for a walk,' I said.

We moved to the start of the ghetto and the hairdressers. 'Over to you, Valentine,' I said.

He took a key from his pocket and opened the door. Inside was a large room at the front with three basins along one wall and mirrors opposite them. The rest of the place was empty save from flyers on the doormat.

'Welcome to your new home,' I said to Buzz.

'I don't understand,' he said.

'I thought we could get a table-tennis table and pool in this room. Maybe a chill-out room at the back by the kitchen for coffee and tea and a place to gather off the streets. Lick of paint might work wonders. Let me know what extra you might need.'

'For us?' he said.

'It comes with two conditions. First, I'll fund you for three months' rent. After that, you have to pay for everything. I suggest you approach some local businesses for support. Should be an appealing PR opportunity for them.'

'And the second condition?' he said.

'You have to share it with the Sharks.'

His face fell.

'Don't despair,' I said. 'We'll help you do a deal with them. This sounds right up Arthur's street.'

'Why are you doing this?' Buzz said.

'Because everybody should get a chance in life,' I said. 'No one should be written off because of their background. Don't let me down.'

* * *

DCI Palmer was shown into my office by Morag. He looked jaded, as though the day had been bad and could only get worse.

'This better be good, Shannon,' he said. 'I'm up to my eyes in Albanians. I don't suppose you know how to speak Albanian.'

'*Nr*,' I said.

'What does that mean?' he said.

'No,' I said.

'Is that all you can say in Albanian?'

'*Po*,' I replied.

'And what does that mean?'

'Yes,' I said.

'You know sometimes you crack me up, Shannon,' he said. 'But not this time.'

Down to business.

'Today's attack on me confirms what we suspect,' I said. 'The only link between Bradley's murder and me is Pym's.

Trying to kill me confirms it. Maybe it's one of the directors trying to force the price down. Maybe it's a fraud. I don't know, but I must be getting close to something.'

'Is Arthur watching you?' Palmer asked.

'Whenever he can. Full time from now on.'

'That's some relief,' he said.

'Did you get anything useful out of the attacker?'

'You mean apart from groans due to his broken hands?' he said. 'No, he's tight-lipped. He's more scared of the person putting out the contract on you than he is of us. He's got a record of unremitting thuggery and some spells in chokey, but is a lowlife in the ecosystem. We've got enough to charge him for GBH and assault, but I think he's a dead end.'

'I've been thinking,' I said.

'Oh no. Not again. It always leads to trouble.'

'I think we made a mistake when searching Bradley's house.'

'We?' he said.

'Well, maybe me,' I admitted.

'That's better. We took his laptop and all his papers. What did we miss?'

'There were some papers on the floor by his chair in the living room — programme guides, quiz books, reading material and so on. We need to get them.'

'If they still exist, that is,' he said. 'What will they tell us?'

'I don't know exactly, but it's the only thing we didn't take. They might provide a clue. Nothing else to do that I can think of. Worth a shot.'

'If they've gone in a rubbish bin and involve a search, you're not going to be very popular,' he said.

'No change there, then,' I said.

'What else do you have for me?' he said.

'We've done a check on most of the key players. There's some expensive cars around, but nothing incriminating. No drug pushers turning up at their homes after work that we could see, but that should be regarded as inconclusive: a couple of the staff smoke weed in the office, so you can see how arrogant they are, and might be evidence of some dealer involved. Not much I can do about that. I could show them the door, but I reckon they'll be out of the picture when we fire Wolfe tomorrow. The panic at the fair means no one has a cast-iron alibi. It was just mayhem. How about your inquiries?'.

'Much the same,' he said. 'We've spoken to all those at the fair — didn't take long — all with the same result. If you were going to murder someone, the fair works in your favour. No one saw anything; no one heard anything bar the screams. How about Pym's? Any fraud going down as a possible motive?'

'You would think so,' I said. 'Love and money would be the two favourite motives. Love of money even better.'

'Grandmothers and egg sucking,' he said.

'One man who was foolish and fell on his sword, but that was before the attempts on my life, so that would rule him out. A couple of things nagging at me that I can't put my finger on. More time might help me find the answer, but who knows? My gut feeling, though, tells me something is going down.'

'Despite everything, I trust your instincts,' he said. 'Keep digging.'

'Will do, although we're almost finished at Pym's. Good luck with your Albanians.'

'I may come back to you, re "no," if I'm desperate.'

'Feel free. I'll keep you posted,' I said.

'Daily,' he said.

'Oh, hellfire,' I said suddenly. 'I've just realised I was supposed to buy a suit today.'

'No problem,' Palmer said. 'There's a Hong Kong tailors called Changs in Bethnal Green. Mention my name, and he'll do a made-to-measure suit in three days. He owes me. Remind him of that. Happy hunting.'

I moved to the conference table and logged into the account system at Pym's. While it was loading, I went through to the river room. Anji and Valentine were sharing a bottle of ice-cold cider, and Cherry something that looked like either a vodka or gin and tonic, slimline almost certainly. When you're that beautiful, you have to put in some work. I took a beer from the fridge and popped the cap. 'Anyone want to join me?' I said as I walked through to my office. All three brought their drinks through.

We sat around the table and waited for something to jump into our minds. I dragged the pile of voucher copies across the table to me and riffled through to the first ad that had printed badly and deserved a refund. I went into the purchase ledger and saw a credit there. I tried with another one. Credit note received. Then I looked at the other credits in the ledger — plenty there with credit notes, too — TV ads where the client's preferences, such as solus in ad breaks, had not been observed. All checked out. Then a thought struck me.

'Come and look at this,' I said.

My three comrades sighed and came to look at the screen.

'Here's the purchases ledger,' I said. 'Here's the same analysis by supplier. What strikes you?'

'They're pretty brutal in getting credit notes,' said Cherry.

'Agreed,' I said. 'What else? Look at their biggest supplier, TVGo.'

Cherry looked and said, 'Ah.'

'What?' said Anji.

'We're agreed on them being brutal on ads that don't meet the specified criteria. Look again. What strikes you now?'

Anji looked more closely at the screen. She looked at Valentine. He nodded.

'A perfect record,' they said in unison. 'Not one credit note.'

'Exactly,' I said. 'And that's where we start tomorrow.'

The cold beer never tasted better.

CHAPTER FIFTEEN

I called in at Changs in Bethnal Green on my way to Pym's, anxious to make progress on the suit as soon as possible so I could heave a sigh of relief and tick that off the wedding to-do list. Palmer's name worked magic and Chang said he'd work all weekend. The fitting took an hour and involved me making strange contortions with my body while Chang flittered around me with a measuring tape. After Chang was satisfied, we got down to a multitude of choices: three-piece or two-piece, the former; main fabric, plain light grey; three buttons on the jacket; two slits at the back; lining, blue; matching handkerchief for top pocket; how many buttons on the sleeve, four; flaps on pockets, yes. It went on and on. While all this was going on, I made a call to Andrew Hamilton, Group Marketing Director at Zeus, whom I had met at the start of the week.

'I need an in to TVGo,' I said. 'Know anyone there with whom I could get a meeting? As high up the tree as possible. It's urgent, and I'd need to talk to the accounts manager, too. If I'm right, it could be very important to them.'

'Fraud?' he said.

'I think so,' I said. 'I need to test a theory, but it's all pointing to something big.'

'I met the Chief Finance Officer on one of the jollies the media owners have. Leave it with me. I'll call you back.'

Mister Chang finished the interrogation and he assured me I could pick it up on Monday, Tuesday at the latest. It was all looking a bit tight, if you excuse the pun. If Chang or the jewellers let me down with the rings or suit, it would be a disaster. I got into the Beamer and drove to Soho, parking in the garage and walking to Pym's. I saw Arthur's white van pull in behind me and felt relatively safe for the first time in a couple of days.

Brookie was waiting for me in reception.

'Come along quickly, Mister Shannon,' she said. 'We were expecting you earlier. Mister Pym has arranged a meeting with Wolfe in ten minutes.'

We scurried to the lift and with much metal jangling, we reached the top floor. We went straight to Pym's office and found him pacing up and down.

'You've spoken to board members about this?' I asked.

'We're all in agreement about this. As you said, there were some sighs of relief. It's a case of "best it were done quickly", or however the quotation goes.'

'How do you want to play this?' I said.

'I'll deliver the valediction if you stand by for fielding questions. I don't know how quickly I'd think in the circumstances. This is so unlike me. See, look at my hands shaking.'

'Any chance of some coffee, Brookie?' I said. 'We might need a special one. Time to get back on track later.'

'Understood,' she said. She went to a glass Cone jug bubbling away on the top of a filing cabinet and began to pour.

The coffee would taste bitter from being stewed, but we wouldn't be having it for the taste. Right now, there were no connoisseurs.

Wolfe came in and Pym asked him to sit down. He was as untidy as when I first met him, with a baggy red sweater over flared denim jeans. He was wearing utilitarian trainers rather than a stylish brand. If this was his idea of dress-down Friday, he'd better look again at his calendar.

'What's all this about, Vernon?' he said. 'Why is Shannon here? This is all very disruptive. I was part way through a new concept for Seeco.'

'No need to worry about that now,' Pym said. 'We had a meeting of the board last evening and came to a conclusion.'

'Why wasn't I there?' Wolfe said. 'How dare you call a meeting without me.'

Vernon took a sip of his coffee and smiled. 'The meeting was about you.'

'What about me?' Wolfe said. 'This is all very underhand.'

'We came to a decision,' Pym said.

'I've had enough of this,' Wolfe said. 'I'm off, till you show me some courtesy.'

'I'd advise you to stay,' I said. 'Better for everybody if this is done in person rather than by a letter or email. That's courtesy, in my book.'

'You can shut up,' he said angrily to me. 'You're always poking your nose in where you have no business.'

Pym took a sip at his coffee and let out the breath he had been holding.

'Enough indeed,' he said. 'As I was saying, we reached a decision. It was felt that it would be in the interests of the business if we parted company.'

'Parted company?' Wolfe said. 'Say what you mean. You're going to give me the sack?'

'We, the directors, have agreed that we will give you three months' salary if you go immediately with no fuss. We feel that is generous, in the current state of the business. Your record of creative output and winning pitches has been holding us back.'

'I won't stand for it,' Wolfe said, his face flushed with temper, veins on his forehead pulsing. 'I'll take you to a tribunal.'

'I wouldn't advise that,' I said. 'One mention of you letting members of your staff smoke weed in the office, and you'll find all credibility lost in an instant.'

I sipped my coffee. Mister Cool. Give Pym confidence.

'I think that about sums it up,' I said.

'I'd be grateful if you could pack your things and go without a final word or activity with your creative staff,' Pym said. 'Please do not say anything to your staff. I will talk to them immediately after this meeting.'

'I'll take some of the teams with me,' he said. 'See how you like that.'

'We will cope,' said Pym.

'And who will you be able to replace me with? Who would want to come to a struggling agency?'

'I have an idea about that,' I said. 'I'll work it up at the weekend, but I think we can put our struggles behind us. What's the time, Mister Wolfe? Time to go.'

He stood up and threw his chair at me in anger. I dodged it easily.

'Nice try; no cigar,' I said.

I picked up the coffee cups, still half-full and gave them to Brookie.

'I don't think we need that anymore,' I said to Pym. 'Right, Brookie. Roll in the creatives.'

Quickly, all five teams came into the office and stood in front of him with puzzled faces. The astute might have caught a glimpse of Wolfe making his exit and guessed the reason for their summons.

'I have to tell you,' Pym said, 'that Mike Wolfe is no longer an employee of this company. We want only loyal staff to stay. If you would like to follow him, we will pay you three months' salary. Think carefully. Who would want to go?'

No hands went up. Not even Tony and Ned. Interesting.

'Then time to get back to work in a revitalised company. Thank you for your support.'

'Not what I was expecting,' I said to Pym, when they had departed. 'There were supposed to be cries of "I am Spartacus!" all around. Give yourself the weekend and Monday to rehearse your stories, then call a press briefing for Tuesday. We need to beat Wolfe to the punch. He'll probably spend the weekend fuming, so that might give us the edge. You need to get your position out there before

Wolfe pours vitriol to the media. You should also start your search for a replacement. Make a list and clear it with the board. You need to act fast.'

My phone rang and I saw Andrew Hamilton's name flash. 'One moment,' I said to Pym. 'I need to take this.'

I answered the call and went up the other end of the room.

'You're in luck,' Hamilton said. 'Meeting set up for one o'clock. Any preferences for sandwiches?'

'Anything that won't cloy in my mouth.'

'Ah,' he said. 'That sort of meeting.'

'Very,' I said. 'Thanks for the introduction. I'll let you know what I can tell you.'

I went back to Pym.

'This has to be a new start. Not just for the business, but for you, too. That's the last whisky to part your lips.'

I opened the door and called in Brookie.

'Vernon has something to say to you,' I said.

'Pour the contents of the whisky bottle down the sink and don't buy another. From now, I'm dry.'

Rebirth.

* * *

I went to our room and looked again at the purchases. I checked then at the sales ledger just to make sure that items had been posted there in error. All correct. I checked again. I wasn't wrong. I checked with my beautiful watch. Time to set off for the meeting.

I exited the building and felt Arthur's eyes roving side to side and back to front. I wondered where he had parked his trusty van. Somewhere illegal, but off the rounds of the traffic warden. TVGo was in Docklands in part of the famous tower of Canary Wharf. I parked the Beamer, having been checked through the entrance. The security guard informed me of the numbered bay where I should park and wrote down my time of entry on a clipboard. Somehow it seemed out of keeping for the guard to have a clipboard: better to have a 9mm hand-gun strung up in a holster on his left side. I decided I had been reading too much American crime fiction and that I should concentrate on the here and now.

TVGo's offices were on the eighth floor. The reception area was modern without the need for special gimmicks. Cool and bright and ready for summer. I caught myself wishing for an early summer. Just let it be dry on the day. Don't let it rain on Cherry's parade.

The receptionist — bright and cheery in a white blouse with a blue neckerchief reminiscent of cabin crew first class: I wondered if under the desk was a pair of red stilettos. She asked me to sit down while I waited to be collected for entry. Very soon, I was greeted by a woman looking like she was waiting for summer, too: she was dressed in a loose-fitting tan jumpsuit with a collection of bead necklaces and armbands. Sophistication: if that was the intention, then she was spot on.

She introduced herself as Catherine, the PA to Hal Armitage. 'Don't use anything but Hal when you're speaking to him,' she advised. 'He believes in informality.'

Well, that was an interesting start, I thought.

She took me to the lift and pressed the button for the twelfth floor. The lift opened to a space for greeting or exiting with double glass doors at the front and back. Or it could be the other way round. Another puzzle.

The whole floor, as promised by reception, was open plan, apart from two doors at the back, and filled with smiling faces and no evidence of classic blue-and-white uniforms. Be yourself. This looked like a good place to work.

Catherine took me to one of doors, knocked out of habit, and opened the door. Inside, a man and a woman stood up. The man was tall and in his late thirties and was wearing a pair of sand chinos with a black T-shirt and a dull red blouson jacket. His hair was black and slightly longer than the current trend. A new trend? I wondered. I could never see this guy off trend.

The woman was short and slim. She was around thirty-five, at a rough guess, and had blonde hair plaited in corn rows like she was back in the eighties with Bo Derek. She was wearing a white skirt, two inches above the knee, with a dark brown vest and cork-soled espadrilles.

They introduced themselves as Hal, which I was already primed to use, and Sandra — "call me Sandy" — Williams. She had a laptop open on the glass-topped table in front of her.

I went through the formalities and sat down next to Sandra — sorry, Sandy, we're informal — and prepared my story.

'Pleased to see you,' Hal said. 'Or should I say honoured. I've read a lot about you, and Andrew Hamilton speaks highly of you. If you needed a PR person, he would fit the role.'

'As you may know,' I said, 'we're looking into Pym's advertising agency at the moment — nothing sinister, just helping with a share placement — and a situation has come up. I've been drilling down on credits issued for press and TV. You seem to have an excellent record. Not one credit note issued in the last six months.'

'I would like to claim that as a record,' Sandy said, 'but it's not true, I'm afraid.'

She tapped and clicked the laptop. 'Three is the correct number,' she said.

'I've looked deeply into the last six months of the accounts and I can't find any refunds in them, or anything hitting the bank.'

'Who's right?' Hal said to her. 'You or Shannon?'

Sandy moved the laptop around so I could see the screen.

'Look into the last column of the situation of Pym's. Three refunds, totalling four hundred thousand pounds.'

'That's a lot of money,' I said. 'What's the reason for it?'

'One of our sales team had billed the wrong package. Billed for the top package, with all the bells and whistles and highest rating programmes, when it should have been the level three package. He's done it three times, and I'm on the verge of reporting him if it happens again. Too much money involved to be lenient.' She brought up a new page on the screen. 'Here you go,' she said. 'You can see the three items coming out of our bank.'

'Something's wrong,' I said. 'Money coming out for you, but not being received by the bank account of Pym's. Can you tell me more about the transactions?'

'Simple,' she said. 'You haven't checked the number two account.'

'There is no number two account,' I said.

Hal had curiosity grabbing him by the lapels. 'I agree with Shannon. Something isn't right.'

'It clearly states that all refunds go to the number two account,' Sandy said. 'Someone must have authorised it. Here you go — authorised by a person in sales.'

It was all beginning to make sense.

'The same person who made the mistakes?' I said.

Sandy clicked away into the further recesses of the accounts. 'Yes, that appears so.'

'Am I on the same page as you?' Hal said.

'I suspect so,' I said. 'We need everything you have on this number two account. We need to track it back to the source. If I'm right, and I think we are now in agreement, yourselves and Pym's have been — let me use a technical term — *diddled* out of four hundred thousand pounds. Can you tell which client was involved in this?'

'Easy,' Sandy replied.

'Don't tell me,' I said. 'I like the drama. Seeco crisps and snacks.'

Sandy nodded.

It was all fitting together.

'Get this man in,' Hal said to Sandy. 'Tell Catherine, and she'll track him down. Meanwhile, who's for a sandwich?'

Catherine brought in a tray of sandwiches and a bottle of red wine. I allowed myself a small glass, to make sure I was below the limit for driving, and put a tuna mayo sandwich on my plate. On further thought, I added a beef and horseradish and a prawn in Marie Rose sauce to it. Spoilt for choice. I could get to like this guy — or should it be Catherine? — for the choice of sandwiches. We sat back, munched, chatted while waiting.

'I'm beginning to think we should hire your services,' Hal said. 'This should never be allowed to happen. We need to sharpen up, Sandy. Give me your recommendations on Monday morning, and, I suspect, join a waiting list for Shannon's services.'

It took fifteen minutes for Catherine to locate the man and he came in with a very worried expression on his face. He knew the game was over.

He was introduced as Wayne Robinson, He was short and rounded by too many expense account lunches. He stood there shuffling from foot to foot — Hal didn't offer him a seat. It was back in the headmaster's study for a caning.

'Tell me about the number two account.' Hal said.

I felt there was bluster coming.

'Allow me,' I said. 'I think the other person in your scam is Richard Cawley.'

Cawley, the media buyer. *Call me Rich, because it's true.* A million miles, in image, from his partner, Emma Potter of the multicoloured hair.

'I'll confirm that later,' I went on, 'when I haul him in before Pym and me. I don't know from where the original idea came to you. The both of you must have assumed that no one would notice or care when you authorised the credit note. Maybe you had to cut in the person responsible for checking on the TV schedule, or maybe you supply him or her with the lower-cost package for the checks. Fill us in, please. Start at the beginning.'

'I caution you,' Hal said, 'that if you lie to us, I will hand you straight over to the Fraud Squad. Tell us the unexpurgated story, and I might not have to get the police involved.'

'It was about five months ago,' he said. 'Richard and I were at one of our jamborees in Marbella. We palled up during a late-night session in some Irish bar and had too much to drink. Richard said, wouldn't it be fun if we fleeced Pym's. It was a bit of a laugh, and Richard said how easy it would be. We agreed we'd test the water — not going for too much in one hit — just twenty thousand. It was my idea to create the number two account and feed it into our system. It went without a hitch.'

'So then you went back for more?' Hal said.

'We agreed that we would stop after three times. Went for one hundred and eighty thousand, and the last one for two hundred thousand. We got worried when Shannon was called in. When Bradley was murdered, we thought that would distract his attention from us. So, what are you going to do?'

'How much of the money is left?' I asked.

'There's about one hundred and fifty thousand of my share. You'd need to talk to Richard about his half.'

'What did you spend the other fifty thousand on?' Hal said.

'I bought a second-hand Porsche 911. Was a bargain.'

'That's nice to know,' Richard said. 'You sell the car and pay back the full two hundred thousand. Every penny. Then I might think about not getting the police involved.'

'That might not be possible,' I said. 'I'm working with the police on the Bradley murder. I would feel morally obliged to report this to the officer in charge. I can't vouch for what he might decide to do. Paying back the money might make a difference.'

'Needless to say,' said Hal, 'you are sacked. Get yourself a large cardboard box, clear your things and be gone by the end of the day. I'll be in touch when I've talked to Vernon Pym. He may well feel he wants the full force of the law brought down on you. It's his money, at the end of the day. Is that right, Shannon?'

'I would think so,' I said, 'but I reckon he would support any action of yours. He's a benevolent man, but I don't know how much this would test his limits. Call him later, Hal, and I'll fill him in with all the details when I get back.

I think we all know what will happen when he learns about Richard Cawley. Everyone should get what they deserve in a just society. It will give me great pleasure to be there when Pym faces him.'

'I'm getting a picture here,' said Hal. 'Likeable man, is he? One of your closest friends. I kind of think I would like to be there, too. But I won't steal your thunder. Well, these sandwiches aren't going to eat themselves.'

A thought struck me. 'What are your thoughts about Pym's and the share sale?'

'Not a good bet with the murder of Bradley unsolved,' he said. 'Clients a bit jittery, I expect. Pitches thin on the ground, too, I would think. Shaky time.'

He took the last roast beef sandwich — damn — while I phrased my answer.

'There is an argument that says exactly the opposite,' I said. 'Buy at the bottom of the market. Creative director gone. Fresh start with someone new? Today they've gone from cash-poor to cash-rich. Assets increased. Sound business again. Sky's the limit, if you excuse the pun knowing the name of competition. Might be a smart move.'

'Going beyond the call of duty, eh, Shannon? Outside your brief. People talk highly of you and respect your opinion. An interesting slant on what may happen. I expect we're going to see a lot of each other in the future. Leave it with me.'

And that's what we did.

* * *

I called Brookie as I was walking to where I'd parked the Beamer. Told her to keep the afternoon free for me with Pym. I didn't look out for Arthur. I knew instinctively he would be following, watching my back, front and sides.

It was half past two when I got back to Soho. I went straight to Brookie's anteroom and checked in on her.

'How's he doing?' I asked.

'Much brighter,' she said. 'He took a call from a Mr Armitage, and that seemed to perk him up.'

'Clear for me to go in?' I said.

'His door is always open to you,' she replied. 'You're such a tonic to have around.'

'Most tonics are false,' I said. 'Medicine-man bottles of things you don't want to know, sold by charlatans moving from one place to another, one step ahead of you.'

'You know,' she said, 'there are times when I don't have a clue what you're talking about, but I trust you.'

Vernon Pym gave me a huge smile when I entered his office. There were no coffee or tea cups visible that might have contained whisky. Things were looking up. I doubted if he would be so jolly when he heard the other side of the coin.

'Well done, Shannon,' he said. 'Armitage has given me the good news. Fill in the detail, please.'

'Quite a simple con, really,' I said. 'Bill the client for a higher package than he has asked for. Appear to rectify the situation. Transfer the difference as a credit note to a fictitious account purporting to be a real account, pocket the difference. In total, it amounted to four hundred thousand pounds. You should check with your insurer to see if fraud is covered, because when you get a credit that should go to Seeco as they are the losers, though you would get your fifteen per cent commission — that's sixty thousand. You should talk to Armitage, too, to see if you can claim on their insurers.'

'How are we looking on your final bill?' he asked. 'Not that I would argue the final amount. I'm very grateful for cleaning the Augean stables.'

'By the end of the week we will have finished our work here, with our valuation, so that's ten days at five thousand pounds.' I let the figure sink in before moving on. 'The ten per cent rate on frauds discovered will be forty thousand pounds on this latest con, and twenty thousand pounds for O'Hara's losses on the advanced payment by the client. Altogether, a sum of one hundred and ten thousand pounds, but on the plus side, there's the sixty grand coming into your coffers.'

'All assuming you don't find anything else in the next week,' Pym said.

'And there's still a link between yourselves and Bradley's death. Be good to clear that up before the end of next week. I'm working with the police, so there's still a real chance of catching the murderer. Never give up hope.'

'I agree,' he said. 'The situation here is moving from black clouds to a light mist that might be broken up by a burst of sunshine, if we ever see it.'

'Any thoughts on the creative director vacancy?'

'All the board members are racking their brains to come up with a short list.'

'Gather all the directors for a board meeting on Monday afternoon, say three o'clock. Not any earlier, as I have a lunch to arrange.'

He nodded. 'Well,' he said. 'I don't suppose we can put it off any longer. Time for a wee chat with Cawley.'

While we were waiting, I called Palmer and told him there had been developments, and that he should call on us later. Oh, and don't forget the papers from Bradley's house. He grunted that was he the sort of person who would forget things?

Good point.

Cawley came in — not quite so Rich today — and sat down opposite Pym and to my right side. The birthmark looked a deeper shade of purple today. Stress-related? He would have spoken to Wayne Robertson and knew what was going to happen. He slid a A4 piece of paper across the desk to Pym.

'My resignation,' he said, making a move to get up.

'Sit back down,' Pym said. 'We have the matter of reparations to discuss. I'll offer the same deal as Robertson got from TVGo. Repay all the money you stole, and I'll not think about getting the police involved. No promises, though.'

'I only have about one hundred and fifty thousand pounds left.'

My heart bled for him.

'I see you have a passion for fast cars,' I said. 'Sell the Lotus. And anything else of value. Watches, rings and so on. You might start now. Pass us the watch. Take off the rings.'

'How did you know about the Lotus?' he said, struggling with a tight gold ring.

'"Always do your homework" is a catchphrase of ours,' I said. 'You'd better keep that in mind when looking for a new job. I don't fancy your chances.'

'It was just a game,' he said. 'See if we could beat the system.'

'And the money was unimportant? Is that what you are saying?' Pym said. 'I despair for you. Don't insult my intelligence or stretch my credibility past its limits. Be gone with you.'

I liked that. Nice phrasing. Very Shakespearean. Straight out of a tragedy. Boo hoo.

Cawley slunk out of the room.

Mission accomplished.

Don't you just love it when a plan comes together?

Beware.

CHAPTER SIXTEEN

I arrived home elated, expecting praise from Palmer. All I got was a black plastic sack and a grunt.

'Here,' he said, placing the sack on the conference table in my office, 'everything in the paper recycling bag. I hope it wasn't the sort of material that needed shredding, otherwise you've got a hell of a jigsaw to complete. As I'm officially off duty, a beer would go down a treat.'

I went through to the river room and took two bottles from the fridge and popped the caps. I got two drip mats to make Palmer feel included in his OCD habit. He rolled his bottle across his forehead, took a sip, sat back and sighed.

'Albanians still causing you troubles?' I said.

'Can't find an expert translator. I'm beginning to doubt anyone exists who can speak Albanian. More than that, I'm beginning to think they don't even speak Albanian in Albania.'

'I presume this is illegal immigrants?'

'Presumption correct,' he said.

'Boat or lorry?'

'Lorry.'

'And how much do these Albanians pay for this five-star service for them only to be dumped on your patch?'

'Ten grand.'

I let out a whistle. 'How many in a lorry?'

'Thirty.'

I let out another whistle, though louder this time. 'So, if my maths are correct, making three hundred thousand smackeroos per trip.'

'Correct again,' he said. 'Big business. Hard to compete with that with the limited resources we have. But let's talk about the subject in hand. What have you got for me? Your message sounded intriguing.'

'I have two suspects,' I said.

'Sounds like a breakthrough,' he said.

'The downside is that I don't think either of them killed Bradley.'

'Why do you always do this to me, Shannon?' he said. 'You dangle the carrot, get me excited and then snatch it away.'

'Two people — one working for Pym's and one for TVGo — have been pulling a scam over the last six months to the total of four hundred grand. It would certainly be enough reason to protect themselves from my usual meddling, but enough to kill Bradley — I don't think so? They were two guys out for a bit of fun as well as for the money. Stick it to the man. You could say they had a motive and the opportunity, because of the pandemonium at the fair. Means? It's not hard to buy a knife.'

'What do you want to do about it?' he said.

'I could pass the names to you, but we did say they were off the hook if they paid back the stolen.'

'So that would mean no honour, my honourable friend.'

'Exactly,' I said.

'I'll give you a little time before pulling them in,' he said. 'You do understand that will put you in deficit in my account? Another favour to repay along the line? You are absolutely sure about this pair?'

'My gut feel is that they're not the sort of people to commit murder.'

'So it's your gut feel against my thirty years' experience as a copper?'

'That's about it, I suppose,' I said.

'No "suppose" about it,' he said. 'If this was my office, I would be saying "Get out of here". But all that's left is for me to finish my beer and get back to the missus for another shrivelled-up dinner.'

He drank the last of his beer.

'Keep me posted,' was his parting shot across my bows.

I pulled in the troops and gestured at the black sack. 'A problem shared is a problem halved,' I said. 'If we all pitch in, it won't take ten minutes to find what we're after.'

'And what are we looking for among this problem halved?' said Cherry.

'I'm not entirely sure,' I said, 'but if my memory serves me rightly, it will be programme guides, quiz books and anything else Bradley might have resorted to for leisure time while sat in his chair.'

'Broad brief,' said Norman.

'Par for the course when you're shaking the tree,' I said. 'Right, folks, dig deep.'

It did only take ten minutes, and we agreed we would work through what we had found in the morning. All but Norman went into the river room. He was restive and strangely disinterested in leaving my office. We said we would join them in a little while. Morag brought in two beers and we sipped in silence for a while.

'You're scared, aren't you?' he said.

'Nothing wrong with being scared when someone is out to kill you,' I said.

'It's not that,' he said. 'You've handled that before. You're scared of the wedding. Admit it.'

'It's a big step,' I said. 'So permanent.'

'That's the whole point of it,' he said. 'Give an oath to love each other as long as you both shall live,'

'What if things change between us?' I said. 'We're happy as we are. Would getting married threaten that? What if giving up a half share in our individual freedoms made us different people?'

'Nonsense,' Norman said. 'You're two people who love each other. Can't be a bigger reason for marriage. I know it must seem overwhelming — the rings, the suit and all the other impedimenta. Cherry so wants a special day. Don't spoil that for her. You can see how much she wants everything to be perfect. You can see, too, how much fun Cherry and Anji are having planning everything to the finest detail. Anticipation is a key. You need that to be seen in a positive mode rather than negative.'

CHAPTER SEVENTEEN

Saturday. Not supposed to be a working day, I know, but the call of Bradley's papers was too alluring, too much promise to ignore. I showered, shaved and dressed in a pair of black jeans and a grey T-shirt. Informal at last. Breathe in the aroma of freedom. I sat at the table in my office with a double espresso and pulled the pile of Bradley's papers in front of me. They were in no particular order, so I sorted them first by date and then, within that, by type — programme guides, TV schedules, puzzle books and what is always called 'miscellaneous' because we can't think of a more intelligent category.

I started with the puzzle books by riffling through their pages. Bradley was a puzzle fiend — crosswords, maths, logic puzzles — commendable, but not always successful. Crosswords not always filled in. Number puzzles not always complete. All my riffling told me was that he liked to exercise his mind, which had a limit. There were no secret messages within their pages.

Next came the programme guides. None of the BBC programmes bore a mark, but the commercial stations had either a tick or a dash against them or were left blank. I remembered from my quick look through a printed sheet that there might be a link to other papers. I found it in the miscellaneous pile. It was headed Seeco and contained a list of advertising slots: ticks and crosses this time. It was abundantly clear. Took not a second to spot. Bradley was checking where and when the Seeco ads were happening. There was one high-rated slot at the beginning, to lull the client into a false sense of security, and then mostly afternoon slots. Bradley knew exactly what was going on. He'd worked out the scam. The payment in cash of two thousand pounds each month was for him to keep quiet. Theorising, he then worked out the scale of the scam and wanted more of the share of the action. And then . . . ?

I made myself another coffee and sat at my desk, debating about the unsocial hours, and called Palmer. He *did* say to keep him posted. Still, I dreaded the response.

What he said was unprintable. He calmed down after I started to explain the need to call.

'Bradley had worked out the media schedule,' I said. 'The people involved and how the scam was operated. He was blackmailing Cawley and Robertson. I think that's enough to pull them in.'

'Honour?' he said.

'We did say "no promises",' I said.

'Fine distinction,' he said. 'Did you have your fingers crossed, too?'

'It's called a moral dilemma,' I said.

'Whatever,' he said. 'The term, in my book, has no meaning. How do I find these people?'

'One of them is called Richard Cawley. I have full details on him from the HR files at Pym's. I'll give you that in a moment. As far as the other guy goes, all I have is that he works at TVGo. No address, I'm afraid.'

'I'll pull in Cawley, and get a contact on Robertson. Are you still sitting on the fence about this?'

'Would you murder someone for a couple of grand a month? I don't think so.'

'I agree,' he said. 'Can't do any harm, though. There's nothing I like better than giving up my weekends to follow your nose. Again, Shannon, keep me posted. Where do I find this Cawley?'

I gave him Cawley's home address.

'Again, keep me posted.'

With that, he cut the call.

I went through to the river room and found Norman and Cherry drinking tea — Cherry's with sophisticated lemon.

'Come and join me, guys. I need your brains.'

We went to my office and sat around the table. I pushed Bradley's material aside and pulled all the working files from Pym's into a neat pile.

'This is where we are now on the share sale,' I said, placing my hand over the pile. 'I'm coming close to a valuation. I'd like you both to look through these and give me your view of the multiple and the profit after tax, in the light of the increase after the return of commission from the media scam. The effect of our bill, too.'

'Which is?' asked Norman, going for the jugular.

'Fifty grand of daily fees and sixty on the ten per cent of frauds recovered — in total, one hundred and ten thousand pounds.'

'Nice work if you can get it,' said Norman, probably singing the song in his head.

'I get the feeling that there's a real chance of turning around the agency. A lot will depend on who they find to take over the pivotal role of creative director. A little housekeeping — watching the head count and general efficiencies due to tidying up the working practices — will help, too. Which leaves us with the problem of the effect Bradley's murder has on the agency — client drift and decrease of invitations to pitch. Pym's needs to boost its image. Could be a shot in the dark, I know, but let me know what you think. Tomorrow would be good. Sorry if that scuppers your weekend, but it's too big a call on my judgement alone.'

'He's getting at you, isn't he?' Cherry said.

'Who?' I said.

'Don't play the innocent with me, Shannon,' she said. 'Pym. That's who.'

'Is this the old story of you siding with the underdog? Heart and head?' Norman said to me. 'David and Goliath? That sort of thing? One lad hassles you to watch your car, and five minutes later, you're running a youth club.'

'I hear what you say,' I said. 'I admit that I've got a vulnerable soft spot, but there comes a time when someone must do something that goes against rationality. To stand up and be counted.'

'Oh, Shannon,' Cherry said. 'Don't ever change. It's one of the reasons why I love you. It's rare to come across anyone with such a heart.'

'At the risk of being a wallflower and getting in the way of your confessions of love,' Norman said, 'but can we get back to today's problem? What do you feel about Vernon Pym?'

'Pym has been running the show for countless years now — "jogging along" might be a better phrase. He made a bad choice when they appointed Wolfe and should have cut their losses earlier. I don't know how much of that was due to Pym or how much was the contribution of the other members of the board. I'd certainly like to be there when they interview the candidates. If there are any candidates, that is. Who would actually want to work at Pym's, knowing the current background? The million-dollar question,' I said.

'Right, Shannon,' Cherry said, 'go do something useful. Take a walk around Island Gardens. Have a drink of watery coffee at the cafeteria. For goodness' sake, give your brain a rest.'

* * *

I was indeed sitting at the cafeteria when the idea came to me. Two ideas, actually, one more easily dealt with than the other. I pulled out my phone and called Campion. OK, it was a Saturday, but we were good friends — more than that: I was the son he'd never had. Remember?

'Meet me at my club on Monday,' he said, 'one o'clock would fit in for me. Wear a tie.'

When I got back, Valentine had arrived. I called him, Anji and Cherry together ready for the big reveal.

'Anyone been a boy scout or girl guide?' I said. 'Or maybe done some orienteering?'

'I was a scout once,' said Valentine, 'but it was a long time ago.'

'What I'm thinking doesn't age,' I said. 'I now know what the import of "McLuhan" was.'

'Do you want a drum roll, Shannon?' said Cherry.

'The medium is the message,' I said. 'I think we have concentrated solely on medium — after all, there was the media scam. What we should have done is think more about the meaning of *message*.' I picked up two voucher copies of the supermarket ads. 'What do you make of these?'

'Pretty standard stuff,' Anji said. 'This week's deals, with no fripperies. Ten-minute job.'

'Look at the code on the coupons. Six digits. Anyone got an idea yet?'

Cherry gave me a raised-eyebrow look. She had got it.

'Just a random selection of numbers,' said Valentine.

'The numbers are there, purportedly, to assess the level of effectiveness of the same ad in different newspapers — work out value for money for each newspaper. Back to the same question. Why six digits, instead of *Daily Mail* one and so on?'

'Are we going to have to drag it out of you, Shannon?' said Cherry.

'To what purpose can a six-digit number be attached?' I said.

'It's a grid reference!' said Valentine triumphantly. 'A grid reference.'

'Exactly,' I said. 'With a four-digit number, you can pinpoint a one- kilometre square on an Ordinance Survey map. With a six-digit reference, you can narrow a location down to a one-metre square. Can't beat that for pinpoint accuracy. Tony and Ned are supplying someone with a location, and, presumably, taking some money in return. That's why they didn't want to leave with Wolfe. We have got them, ladies and gentleman. Oh, how I'm going to love the moment I take them down. Valentine, find us the locations of the code numbers on these two ads. And then . . . Anyone for some exploring?'

* * *

The first location was an abandoned runway on an ex-wartime airfield in Essex. On the journey, we listened to some piano jazz by Fats Waller and Dave Brubeck, two of my favourites, although they had distinctly different styles. It went quickly, but not quickly enough, with the cries of Anji going 'Are we there yet?' The first time it was funny, but got increasingly annoying with every repetition. I turned the volume on the stereo up to attempt to block her out, which was equally annoying for the other passengers. Some days you just can't win.

The airfield was tucked away five miles off the Essex coast, with the nearest civilisation being Southend. It was approached by a heavily potholed tarmac track, which made me scared of the damage it might do to the tyres of the Beamer. There was a dilapidated hangar, a conning tower with a torn windsock and a flat-roofed single-storey building, which I took to be the operations centre.

We got out of the car and stretched our legs. It was a bleak landscape, made even less inviting by a cold east wind that was raw to the bone with each gust. I entered the building, which confirmed my view that it was an office, although that was the only building on site that could perform such a function. Parts of the room had fallen through, and the tiles lay scattered on the floor. The office furniture — a desk and two chairs and a local map on a pinboard — was still there, and I was reminded of the Mary Celeste, wondering if I would find an unfinished meal somewhere. Out of habit, I opened the desk drawers and searched for any evidence of its past life. I found nothing. The floor was back to the bare concrete, and was littered with cigarette butts and wrappers from bags of crisps and other snacks redolent of Seeco, although that brand had only been around in the last few years. There was a toilet in one corner with a washstand; a filthy towel ready in another corner. I lifted the lid on the toilet: it was gross, but interesting, since its contents were still there.

Cigarette butts, toilet tissue and modern crisp packets all pointed to one thing — the office had been recently used. I next went to the hangar and found Anji just coming out.

'I found this,' she said, handing me a newspaper. It was in some foreign language. 'Look at the date. Last Wednesday.'

'Anything else?' I said.

'Cigarette butts, black tobacco, probably Turkish,' Anji said. 'Wrapper from a chocolate bar, also in a foreign language.'

'I think it's time we got going,' I said. 'I don't like sticking around here too long.'

We found Cherry and Valentine and I ushered them in the car. Anji and I got in and we were off.

'What do the grid references say for the other location?' I said.

'Head for Margate,' Valentine said. 'I'll get you something you can put in the satnav in a moment.'

I reported the findings of Anji and me, which had no gasps of astonishment.

'Why are we going to the second grid reference?' said Cherry. 'We all know what this means. We've stumbled across people trafficking. What further evidence do you need to call Palmer?'

'I want to be doubly sure,' I said. 'Palmer can be a hard guy to convince.'

'Poppycock, Shannon,' Walker said. 'You want kudos. The thrill of the limelight. If you must persist, can we not find a welcoming pub somewhere where we can have a half-decent lunch?'

'Your wish is my command, Walker,' I said. 'Let's see what we can find.'

The road to Margate meant coming back towards London and then heading out in the opposite direction. It would give us a break and time to consult before arrival at the second location. After ten minutes, we came to a large pub off the main road before the motorway and pulled in. The place was empty. We were about to discover why.

The inside was dark and gloomy. It would have done much to combat the atmosphere and the chill if the landlord or landlady had actually lit the massive fire in the middle of the room. The interior looked like it was from the eighteenth century, and no one had done anything to it since then. The furniture was brown and large, and the wall were stained nicotine yellow. We sat at a round table with a window to watch the traffic pass. We all knew, inside us, that it would be a disaster.

I went to the bar and ordered drinks and picked up menus. 'No hot food today,' the man behind the bar said. 'My wife's got trouble with her piles.'

Thanks for sharing.

Having ordered our drinks, we felt we might as well test the sandwiches while we drank. The choice was limited, but we cobbled together a plate of tuna mayo, ham and mustard, and cheese and pickles. The best said about them was that they were not curling up. How can you get ham and mustard wrong?

'I'm going to get you for this, Shannon,' Walker said.

'I thought nothing less,' I replied. 'Let's see if we can get some fish and chips in Margate.'

'Shouldn't be too difficult,' Walker said.

'So have we all got the reading from our little adventure in the Essex marshlands?'

Silence meant yes — or complete indifference. Problem solved, so why persevere?

'We've stumbled across people trafficking, haven't we?' Anji said.

'Looks that way,' I said. 'Whoever is behind it is cagey. The traffickers choose a different drop-off point each time, so as not to set a pattern. They make their choice at the last moment, for added secrecy. Tony and Ned give the location by the grid reference in the supermarket ad. I'll call Palmer when we get back. Should solve his Albanian problem, and maybe Bradley's murder, too, if it's connected.'

'You like him, don't you?' Valentine said. 'He's not just a police officer in your book.'

'He's a solid guy,' I said. 'And the world always needs solid guys. He's fun, too, ripe for the harvest of his OCD, but he gives as much as he takes. He's smart underneath the weary facade he puts on about his age and retiring. And, above all that, he trusts me. Can't say fairer than that. He's avuncular, like police officers used to be.'

'What will he do when you give him the news later?' said Anji.

'Cut me some slack, I hope,' I said. 'The ads go in on a Thursday. He'll need to hold his fire until then, when we decode the grid references. Or better still, maybe I can get a look at the artwork before the ad hits the presses. Then it's a case of lying low until the drop-off is made. It won't be the easiest stake-out: if the next location is as barren as last, there won't be many places to hide. We do our bit, and then wait for Palmer to spring the trap.'

'At least we know who is responsible for the attacks on you. The traffickers have all the funds, all the means, to put that together,' Walker said. 'In the end, Bradley's murder had everything to do with the case. They didn't allow for a seasoned map reader to spot the link.'

'It sounds to me,' Anji said, 'like it's two steps forward and one step back.'

'No,' I said. 'The pieces are out of the box. By the end of next week, we can fit them all together in the jigsaw.'

'All done before the wedding,' Walker said. 'Perfect. I've looked at the weather forecast for the day and it's due to be dry. That would be mean we could have the ceremony out-side. Just think of those pictures! Wonderful.'

'What are you going to wear?' I asked Valentine.

'I'm not sure,' he said. 'I only have three suits, and they're all really for business purposes — blue, black, dark grey. Too sombre for a happy occasion.'

'I think we should get you to Chang's first thing Monday. Pull another favour and get you sorted out by Friday. I've gone for classic light grey, if you want to see us matched.'

'So exciting,' Anji said. 'I can't wait.'

We were not far from Margate, and the satnav pointed us to rural roads, and then we ventured off on a track. At the end of the track was a remote farmhouse with a dilapidated roof with only half able to keep out any rain. We got out of the car and spread out. I took the farmhouse, and Cherry, Anji and Valentine went to explore the series of outbuildings.

Inside the barn were discarded wrappings of sandwiches on the floor, some not fully eaten. There was no mould on them and, therefore, were recent. Is that all you get for your ten thousand pounds? There was a desk and two chairs. I opened the drawers of the former. The bottom one was empty, but the top drawer had a collection of bills, all unpaid and in the red zone. Whoever this farm belonged to had either been evicted or just cut their losses and ran. Life for a farmer was beyond difficult, made worse by the supermarkets squeezing every last pip when setting the price of a tomato. Eventually, a developer would buy the land and stick on dozens of town houses and flats. It can be a cruel world.

There was nothing else of interest, so I went outside and met the others.

'Large barn,' Anji said. 'A collection of rotting hay bales giving off a strong rancid smell. Rats running about with perfect nesting sites among the bales. Not the place to come, day or night, if you had a weak stomach or suffered from an Orwellian fear of rats.'

Valentine reported on his search. 'Milking parlour with forty positions. Would have coped with a lot of cows when functioning. Now it seemed empty and without purpose.'

'Place where they used to make cheese,' said Walker. 'Some still there and dissolving with mould. Heady aroma, just like Anji described. This place wasn't empty long.'

'Cigarette butts?' I asked. 'The office had some on the floor — black Turkish tobacco.'

'Same here,' Walker said.

'None from me,' Valentine said.

'Some in the barn,' Anji said. 'Probably to compete with the rotten bales.'

'We've seen enough,' I said. 'Time for that fish and chips.'

'And they have an amusement park there,' Valentine said. 'Maybe we could try some of the rides.'

'Do they have a ghost train?' I asked.

'Looks like it,' Valentine said.

'In that case, I might pass,' I said.

'Me, too,' Walker said. 'Maybe we can sit on the beach while you youngsters get your fix of action and get your adrenaline level up to maximum. I'm starving. Let's fulfil that first and move on from there.'

There was a bewildering choice of places for fish and chips. It was gone three o'clock before we were walking along the prom. Restaurants were shutting up shop for an hour or two before being ready for the evening trade. It made our choice easier. We settled down at a place that looked jolly, with seating outside as well as in. A smiley girl who looked like she was alone at the time took our order of fish and chips all round. She led us to a table for six indoors where we could spread out.

'I hate to be a wet blanket,' Anji said, 'but aren't we all in a precarious position? Maybe even more so now that we've worked out the mechanics of the trafficking business? You said yourself, Nick, that every consignment is worth three hundred thousand pounds to whoever is running the show. Our future is bound up to a solving a grid reference and getting that to Palmer before we are uncovered. If Palmer can't get the lead man, we might have to spend our future looking over our shoulders. This fish and chips is great, by the way.'

'Good to know,' I said. 'The fish and chips bit, that is. For the rest, we do what the mafia calls "going to the mattresses". You all stay at home — which is fortressed by all the safety gadgets that Norman got installed — and only come out when strictly necessary. Arthur can keep following us when we go outside. Palmer needs to hold fire till Thursday. He can't provide police protection without blowing our cover. I agree with you, Anji, the fish and chips is excellent.'

'Stop changing the subject, Shannon,' Walker said. 'The upshot is that we are still targets.'

'Only for next week,' I said. 'By that time, the traffickers will be caught and we'll be finished at Pym's. From then, back to normal.'

'It's a very strange normal nowadays,' said Walker. 'Wherever we go, we seem to be targets. Is that the business plan we all signed up for?'

'I'm happy to go along with it,' said Anji. 'I can't think of a better place to work. It's all thrills. You never know what's going to happen. We uncover scams, send criminals to jail and put the world to rights. As Nick would say, there is honour in what we do. Who else would try to make a success out of two gangs of bored teenagers in a war of knives?'

'I agree,' said Valentine. 'I volunteer to manage the youth club project. I think I can work with them well.'

'All sorted?' I said.

Silence. No objections.

'Let's go and make Palmer's day.'

* * *

If Palmer didn't like me calling on a Saturday morning, he was even less thrilled on a Saturday evening. He scowled at me on arrival. 'Beer?' I said, to break the ice.

'Seeing as I seem to be on perpetual duty, courtesy of you, I'd better not. So why have you summoned me in this time? Column of numbers not adding up?'

'On the contrary, all the numbers add up.'

'Am I going to have to tease it out of you, Shannon?' he said, with a sigh.

'Let me tell you a story. Are you sitting comfortably? The story starts with an arrogant creative team. Each week, they make a boring press ad of latest offers from a supermarket — this weekend's cut-price deals. Somehow, they've got into bed with a bunch of traffickers — probably something to do with a drugs habit. Whatever. It doesn't matter. The press ads go in a range of newspapers, and each carries a different coupon number to see what paper is best value for money. Unlike the rest, the ad in the *Daily Mail* has a six-digit number. Are you with me so far?'

'Six digits,' he said. 'A grid reference. Impressed, Shannon?'

'You've spoilt my big reveal,' I said.

'Once a boy scout, always a boy scout,' he said. 'Be prepared. Good motto for a police officer. Where do these grid reference lead us?'

'We checked up on the latest two. One led to a wasteland that had been used long ago as an airport for amateur planes and lessons, and the other to an abandoned farm. My theory is that the illegal immigrants are brought over in a truck — hopefully, in one of the type that has a fan on the roof — thirty of them packed in. Then the driver reads the coupon in the *Daily Mail*, which tells him where to unload. They all get out and are fed into a coach, then they're off to be dropped somewhere in London, including your manor. You were picked last time as the local lucky winner, hence your Albanian problem.'

'So what's the plan?' he said.

'With a bit of luck and stealth, I can find the coupon number on the previous evening by looking at the artwork, which will be sent to the newspapers and give you the location of the drop-off. Then you lie in wait, which is tricky, because the locations we looked at were isolated: it will not be easy to remain undiscovered. The other problem is that I might know the location, but I won't know the day.'

'As you say, tricky,' he said. 'I know one thing . . .'

'Which is?'

'I've changed my mind about the beer. Just the one, with a glass and a drip mat.'

I went through to the river room and got two beers from the fridge, popped the caps, got glasses and drip mats and returned to my office. Palmer was looking at the mess of papers on the table.

'Are these them?' he said, waving the supermarket ads.

I nodded.

'I better take them.'

'As long as you don't show anyone. These traffickers have a mass of money, and may have informants among the police. If anyone sees them, then our cover is blown and they'll just switch to another way of unloading.'

'If, as you say, the locations are isolated, then it would be strange to see a big truck on a rural road. Let me think it through.' He poured beer into his glass with a faraway look in his eyes. He took a sip. 'Nice beer,' he said. 'Good after a hard day chasing Albanians. Or any other nationality, to that matter.'

'How did you get on with my two fraudsters?' I asked, to fill in the gap while he was forming a plan.

'Your gut feeling was right,' he said. 'They're not murderers. I turned them over to the Fraud Squad, let them have some fun.' He sipped at the beer.

'You're sure of this?' he said.

'Absolutely,' I said, nodding my head.

'You want to be in at the kill?'

I nodded again.

'Consider it done.'

CHAPTER EIGHTEEN

Arthur and I went for a run on Sunday morning. We went through the foot tunnel to Greenwich and did laps around the park. It was still only nine o'clock, but there were tourists up and about to make the most of the fine spring day. We came back and did three laps around Island Gardens to wind down before sitting outside the café, leaning back and letting the sun fall on our faces.

'How's Buzz getting on?' I asked.

'They've started painting, and the place looks brighter,' he said. 'I'm going down there this afternoon, if you want to join me.'

'Will do,' I said. 'Are they still practising the self-defence?'

'They do that at the start of each day,' he said. 'Actually getting quite good at it. I'm pleased.'

'And the Sharks?'

'Blending in nicely,' he said. 'Both sides have recognised that they're not too different to one another. The pool tables and the table-tennis table should be delivered on Wednesday, and I gave them some money for necessities such as a kettle and tea, coffee, milk and sugar.'

'Valentine has volunteered to be project manager,' I said. 'Are you happy with that? Can he cut the mustard, whatever that means?'

'He's the closest of us to their age, so there might be good rapport all round. He's found his niche in life among us. He's a whole different person to the one we first met on the gambling job. Is his dad still pleased?'

'As Punch, as they say. Whatever that means, again. How can hitting your wife on the head with a plank of wood and losing a string of sausages to a crocodile make anyone pleased? Still, sometimes you just have to go with the flow and stop asking questions. Anyway, I think his father is proud of him and how he's carved out a path for himself.'

'Coming up to the end of his three months' probation,' Arthur said. 'Any doubt in your mind?'

'Not an inch. Frankly, we need as many hands as we can get to cope with the workload. Hopefully, when the wedding is over, we can get Cherry and Anji back full time.'

'How are you feeling about the wedding now? Norman said you had a heart-to-heart with him.'

'You're not offended, I hope?' I said. 'Norman was just around when I was at my most melancholy.'

'No offence taken,' he said. 'But you didn't answer my question.'

'I'm scared,' I said. 'This wedding is so important to Cherry. It has to go without a hitch or her dreams will crumble. This is her big day and everything has to be perfect. What are you going to wear? It will be strange to see you in anything bar your donkey jacket.'

'I do have a suit, but I only wear that for funerals. It will have to do. Even Mr Chang couldn't magic me up something made-to-measure in the space of a few days. Probably wouldn't have enough cloth, for a start. I doubt what I wear will be on Cherry's spreadsheet. It will certainly be strange having two best men.'

'There was no way that I could choose between you and Norman.'

'If it makes any difference to your qualms,' he said, 'just think what Arlene would have wanted you to do. "Be happy" is the answer. It's as simple as that.'

'No rest for the wicked,' I said, getting up. 'Time to head back for a shower and spruce myself up for the day ahead. Some big decisions to make later.'

'Meet up about three?' Arthur said.

'Couldn't be better,' I said. 'I may well need a distraction by then.'

* * *

'Would someone like to summarise?' I said as Cherry, Norman and I sat in the river room with coffee.

'Allow me,' Cherry said. 'Pym's is jogging along, nothing better. Its revenue is marginally down, but there's a downward trend there. Wolfe has caused them a lot of lost profit. It strikes me that advertising is a bit like water skiing — if you stop going forward, you sink down. In the last year, they made only a hundred thousand pounds after tax. Almost nothing for a business their size.'

Norman and I nodded our agreement.

'If that wasn't disappointing enough,' Cherry continued, 'we have Bradley's murder to contend with, and Wolfe's departure. Confidence in the business couldn't be lower. They need a shot of something potent in their arm, and they need it quickly.'

'Cash flow is bad,' Norman said. 'Not much cash in the bank, and that's before our invoice of a hundred and ten thousand pounds wipes it out. We can do some clever stuff, such as selling all the cars to a leasing company and then leasing them back, but that will only be a sticking plaster.'

'Are we all agreed on a multiplier?' I said. 'Five is my best estimate.'

'My thoughts, too,' said Cherry and Norman in unison.

'So,' I said, 'valuation of half a million. Might be considered dirt cheap, if it weren't for the latest disruptions. I'm left thinking how we can build confidence?'

'You wouldn't have mentioned it,' said Cherry, 'if you didn't have an answer.'

'Two answers, actually,' I said. 'I'm having lunch with Sir Gerald Campion tomorrow. I hope to persuade him to take a twenty per cent stake in Pym's. That would boost confidence. If Campion views it a good bet, then others — clients and potential clients — will feel the same.'

'You said two answers,' Cherry said. 'The other one?'

'How would you like to own a slice of an advertising agency?'

Silence.

'You can't be serious,' Cherry said.

'No,' said Norman, 'this could all make sense. If we buy a share, then that would be another boost in confidence. It would say to the advertising world that after our due diligence, we regard Pym's as a sound investment. That would affect the multiplier. Could go straight to a multiple of eight. What was half a million would suddenly be worth eight hundred thousand pounds. Add in a new creative director — and Pym's would now look like a better proposition in the market — we can generate higher revenue and profits. There's method in your madness.'

'I'll take that as a compliment,' I said. 'If all goes well with Sir Gerald, we can have a press conference on Tuesday announcing a new structure. I'll get Pym to hold a board meeting tomorrow and see who would now like to buy some shares. It would be good to hold back, say, five per cent for the new creative director.'

'Sounds like a plan,' Cherry said.

'That's good, because I would like you to present it,' I said. 'I can't go blowing my own trumpet talking about what is essentially the Shannon brand. It would be immodest. Maybe even a bit cocky. You have the right tone for this. It would be good, too, for you to take a break of a couple of hours from the wedding planning.'

'I like the idea of a Shannon brand,' said Norman. 'It opens up a whole new revenue stream. We should develop this.'

'One step at a time,' I said. 'There's still Bradley's murder to solve and some traffickers to catch. Be a busy week.'

'Do you have any clues to help catch the murderer?' said Cherry.

'Oh, I know who did it,' I said. 'Proof is another matter.'

'And we have to wait for the big reveal?' she said.

'Exactly,' I said. 'Don't spoil the fun. Be patient. It will all come together in time.'

'Hallelujah,' said Norman.

* * *

Valentine and I met Arthur at the youth club. Arthur was smiling, and rightly so. What was once a hairdressers was being transformed into a cool hangout for the neighbourhood teenagers. There was a tray at the door where the kids had to deposit any weapons before being allowed entry. In time, we wouldn't need the tray. That was the hope. The walls were freshly painted a bright yellow, increasing in light by reflections from all the mirrors.

Buzz came up to us. 'What do you think?' he said with pride. 'Fridge should be arriving tomorrow and electricity connected.'

'How have you managed so far without electricity?' I said.

'No problem,' said Buzz. 'Our boffin, Brains — nerdy but nice — rigged up a feed from the lamppost.'

Exactly what I didn't want to hear.

'You need to disconnect that before tomorrow,' I said. 'I am expecting reporters to be crowding around here jostling for photos. If I'm right, you will make the news. You'll need sponsorship to make it work. I'll give you an intro, then the rest is up to you. And don't forget school. Be bad if you just use this as an alternative to school. Sponsorship will be conditional on school.'

There was a commotion at the door. One youth was refusing to deposit his knife. Part of him, he had said. Never went anywhere without it.

Buzz went over to reason with him. It didn't work. Out of instinct, I guessed, Buzz picked a knife from the tray and faced him off. I had to intervene.

'Put the knife down, Buzz,' I said. 'We haven't spent days teaching you self-defence for you to pick up a knife at the earliest problem.'

Buzz passed the knife to me. I placed it in the tray. I turned to the youth with the knife.

'You,' I said. 'Do you want to spend the best part of your life in prison? Because if you carry a knife, it means you might use it. Life is about honour. You must have a moral code. Never make the first move. Give your opponent a chance to reflect. Don't meet fire with fire. Be confident that you can end this without a fight. Never attack a man that is down, unless it is the only course open to you. Always act with honour, so that you can look at yourself in the mirror and not be ashamed of what you see. Always do what is right rather than what is easy, what is instinctive. Let honour guide you. Drop the knife.'

There were four of us surrounding him, so he let the knife fall from his hand. The real test would be if it was one on one.

'Listen, all of you,' I said. 'You have a chance to change your lives. Build a ladder to the stars and climb on every rung.'

CHAPTER NINETEEN

I called in on Chang and picked up the suit. I could get used to this made-to-measure living, and resolved to sort out my wardrobe when the hiatus caused by the wedding was over. I parked up at the garage and walked to Pym's. Arthur was a shadow behind me.

I went straight to Brookie, and she let down the draw-bridge to allow me to pass through to see Pym. We had some chit-chat about our relative weekends and got down to business.

'I have a plan,' I said. 'The share placement can go through, but I need to know what shareholding you want to keep. What are your thoughts?'

'Twenty per cent would suit me fine,' he said, 'but my ultimate plan was always to sell the lot and retire gracefully. I've not made a secret of that. Twenty per cent would only be a staging post, and would provide me with an element of control, but would give up enough to get the members of the board to feel they had power over their own destinies. What's the plan? It would need to something radical to get us out of this current mess.'

'Do not fear,' I said. 'I specialise in radical. The plan comes in two parts and isn't quite finalised as yet, but will hopefully be after lunch. You have a confidence problem that needs to be solved immediately. The first part of the plan, for which I have approval from the interested parties at Shannon Investigations Limited, is that we take twenty per cent of the shares. That should say to the advertising world that after our due diligence, we feel the agency has a bright future. Are you with me so far? Is that something you can support?'

'And how much control would you assert?'

'Strictly arm's length,' I said. 'I'd like to have one of my colleagues come in and sort out your accounts and your cash flow — housekeeping, nothing else. I'd also like to sit in on the interviews for a new creative director, but that's as far as it goes.'

'I could work with that,' Pym said. 'What's the other part of the plan?'

'I am having lunch today with Sir Gerald Campion — friend, client and chairman of Zeus. I am hoping to persuade him to take twenty per cent, too. Again, it will signal confidence in the agency, that Pym's has a healthy future. Can you live with that, too?'

'When you say radical, you sure mean it,' he said. 'What sort of control would he want?'

'Arm's length again, although I would think he would like to put a non-executive director on the board.'

'Sounds reasonable,' he said. 'To be honest, I wouldn't expect less with such a large shareholding. What do you want me to do?'

'Call a board meeting for three o'clock to see who's on board with these plans, and to determine what shareholding they would want and can afford. Call a press conference tomorrow to announce the changes. Whoever are the key influencers in the advertising industry, they need to be present. Then gear yourself up for a raft of applications for the post of creative director.'

'Will this settle the problem of Bradley's murder?'

'That will be sorted by the end of the week. Trust me.'

'Let's shake on it,' he said. 'Deal done.'

* * *

Campion's club had a discreet entrance off Pall Mall, so discreet that I walked past it at first. The door was painted jet black and a man in a suit with tails opened it for me. He had a stocky build and looked like he had served as a sergeant major in the army. He directed me to a kiosk for me to sign in. It was like going back two centuries in time. An ornate staircase rose up and then divided in two. The ceilings had chandeliers, and there was a lot of detailing around the top of the walls and wood panelling waist high. I was directed to the dining room on the ground floor, where Campion stood up and shook my hand.

'I can't wait till Saturday,' he said. 'I never expected to be invited to the wedding.'

'You are part of our lives,' I said, 'Cherry and me. Wouldn't be right if you weren't there.'

'Let's order,' he said. 'The potted shrimps and roast leg of mutton are always good.' He made a minute gesture with his hand and an observant waiter appeared as if by magic. I went with Campion's suggestion. Would have been rude not to, and I was curious. I hadn't had mutton for many years and wanted to know if it was as good as I had remembered or was seeing it through rose-tinted glasses. We each had a small glass of the house claret to wash it down.

'How is the work for Pym going?' Campion said. 'I suppose I should ask, what are the ramifications of the murder? Damned bad luck.'

'That's one of the matters I wanted to talk to you about.'

'Out with it, Shannon, my boy. How much do you need?'

'I'm recommending the share placement goes ahead, even though confidence is at rock bottom. Pym's needs to reinvent itself or it will slide into obscurity. We're talking phoenix, rebirth and epiphany territory. We're intending to take twenty per cent of the equity. If we are taking twenty per cent, then that must be a signal that Pym's is an agency on a sound financial position, and is now on the way up.'

The potted shrimps arrived. Basically, the shrimps were just a vehicle for half a pound of butter. It came with melba toast and, I had to admit, was delicious.

'How would you like to be part of that journey?' I said.

'As I said, how much do you want?'

'It will be an even bigger signal of confidence if you are on board. It's a good investment — you will be buying at a multiple of five, and with you and me investing, the multiple will increase to eight. I'm proposing a current value of half a million — just petty cash in your terms — and that you and I each take twenty per cent. An outlay of a hundred grand each will immediately become worth a hundred and sixty thousand pounds. Sure-fire winner. I wouldn't put our money in if I thought there was any chance of a loss. Together we can ramp up confidence and turn the business around.'

'So all you want for the twenty per cent is a hundred grand? A tick on an elephant's hide. Talk to David Shapiro; it'll give him a chance to subtly introduce Valentine into the conversation and see how his son is getting on. Shapiro will put forward someone to talk to the press. Ah, the roast mutton.'

A silver-domed trolley arrived, and the lid opened to reveal a joint of mutton that got the gastric juices flowing. The waiter carved two thick slices each and set them on warmed plates. He added roast potatoes and placed them before us, then a little jug of gravy and some Cumberland sauce. Another waiter set out a dish of mixed vegetables in the middle of the table.

'I told you it was good,' Campion said.

We dined with sighs of pleasure until time was ripe for my second favour.

'I've got myself involved in a project,' I said.

'How much?' he said again.

'More petty cash for you, but let me fill you in with the details. Not far from your office is a dismal area of run-down flats and empty shops. In this depressing atmosphere is a group of teenagers about to be sucked into a life with no promise for the future. I'm trying to give them a break, something that will give them hope. We've taken over an empty hairdressers and are making it into a kind of youth club. Valentine is overseeing it. If you became one of the sponsors, it will be good PR.'

'We have a department that deals with such matters. It's called community and social responsibilities, although I couldn't swear to that, as they keep changing the name. Let me give you a name.'

He took out a diary from his jacket pocket, got out a pencil from the little loop along the side and wrote a name on it. He added the main switchboard number and passed the note to me.

'How much of all this is heart — the Shannon soft spot — and how much is head?' he said.

'I can't deny that I feel for these kids. If I don't do something, most of them will be in trouble with the law within the next few years. I would feel like I was abandoning them. I wish I hadn't got involved, but I did and to leave them as they are would be turning a blind eye to the problem. I think they're a good bunch inside. They just need a way to let that shine through.'

'And what about Pym's? The same question: head or heart?'

'Purely head. There's some nice people there, too, but they lost their way. One bad appointment, and that started a slow fall in profits. There's potential in Pym's. Get the right creative director and they're back on course. It's a sound investment.'

'Let's talk no more of business,' he said. 'Are you getting nervous about the big day? Is losing focus and thinking of business an easy escape for you? Avoiding the issue?'

'Possibly,' I said. 'But Cherry's got everything sorted out and has no need for my input. I've talked to Arthur and Norman — you'll love them when you meet them on Saturday — and done the heart-to-heart. I think I'm sorted now. Any nervousness is only natural. Nerves get the adrenaline going, and is helpful to function at your best.'

'Sounds more like a battle than a wedding,' he said.

'I'm sure it will be fine,' I said casually. 'Cherry has everything planned out to the finest detail. So much so, it does smack of a military campaign. As long as they open the bar as soon as us men arrive, then everything will be OK.'

'Time for us to return to making money,' he said, shaking my hand. 'Good to talk to you. See you Saturday. You can uncross your fingers now.'

* * *

The board of Pym's were assembled when I got back. Cherry was there at the head of the table, Pym opposite her at the other end and Brookie had her notebook ready to take the minutes of the meeting. The directors spread around. They were, according to the briefing notes I had given her:

Des Hawkins — media director.

Fiona McCloud — newly appointed finance director.

Paul Adams — accounts director.

Harry Barker — head of planning.

I nodded at Cherry and smiled to signify all had gone according to plan. I took a seat next to her and slyly touched her hand. *Over to you.*

'Lady and gentlemen,' she said. 'I will be chairing this meeting for reasons that will become clear as we proceed. I have a proposition to put to you. An opportunity that is too good to resist.'

She took a sip from a glass of water, which was as much about increasing the tension and drama as to do with the dry mouth she must have had. Nerves get us in different ways, but dry mouth is universal.

'We — Shannon Investigations Limited — have valued the worth of Pym's as half a million pounds. This is at the very bottom of the market because of the uncertainties of the current problems — Bradley's murder and having no creative director — as well as lacklustre past performance. Each per cent of the offer price will, therefore, be equivalent to five thousand pounds. We would put forward this view in terms of a multiple of five times. When all the restructuring of the business is put forward, the worth of the agency will be valued at a multiple of eight, due to eliminating the uncertainty that is currently surrounding it.

'How do we instil the necessary confidence? Vernon has decided to relinquish shares so as to leave him with twenty per cent of the business. And now comes the clever bit — in two parts, actually. We — Shannon Investigating Limited, widely recognised as financially astute and the cure for many financial problems, a stamp of approval — will take up twenty per cent of the business. Because of the power of the Shannon name, and Shannon himself, too modest to lead the discussions today, it will signal that Pym's is not only a going concern, but has potential to grow. Without these factors, then we would not be investing. All clear so far?'

No one needed any clarification.

'Now the second part. Discussions have taken place with Zeus to acquire twenty per cent of the shares. If Zeus is getting involved, then everything must be of the highest standard and of long-term rewards. The second boost to confidence. That, lady and gentlemen, leaves forty per cent of the shares available to you. We are thinking of five per cent each of the shares, an outlay of twenty-five thousand pounds, the rest held back for future investment and a share for the new creative director when he or she proves his or her worth. We need to know whether you are on board or not. The floor is open.'

'I'm too new into a position that may only be temporary,' Fiona said. 'A later date for me would be better.'

'I'm in,' said Hawkins. 'I'll take ten per cent, if it's going.'

'I'm in, too,' said Adams. 'Ten per cent will suit me as well.'

'And another vote for ten per cent for me,' said Barker.

'Excellent,' said Cherry. 'That would leave ten per cent for later distribution and for a creative director. I declare this meeting closed.'

* * *

'That went well,' I said to Cherry as we drove back. 'Well done, Walker. Nicely handled.'

'Now we can get back to matters of high interest,' she said.

'The wedding?' I said.

'The wedding,' she said. 'How are the speeches going?'

Speeches!

'In hand,' I lied.

'Have you spoken to Norman and Arthur about their speeches?'

'Not quite,' I said.

'What does that mean?' she pressed.

'Well. Actually . . .'

'You haven't spoken to them, have you?'

'No, but I meant to.'

'And your speech?' she said.

'I've got some ideas,' I said.

'Oh, Shannon,' she said. 'When we get back I'm going to lock the three of you in your office with a drink and a A4 pad, and no one comes out till they've finished.'

'Better make it a large vodka over ice and threaten it from six yards away with orange juice,' I said.

She was silent. I searched for something positive.

'I do have the suit now,' I said.

'Thank heaven for that,' she said. 'I won't have to see you waiting for me in the aisle in your underpants.'

'They are nice underpants,' I said.

'That may be so,' she said, 'but they won't be getting a visit from me until the speeches are done.'

My silence this time.

CHAPTER TWENTY

The press briefing on Tuesday went without a hitch. Zeus had sent a representative from their PR department and, with more experience than either me or Pym's, we let him run the show. Reactions from the journalists were initially surprise, and then they were impressed by the plans we had put together. The shares bought by myself were something different, although similar deals had been done over the years, and the clean bill of health from our involvement was positive. The investment by Zeus further emphasised that the business was on a new trajectory and would be going places. And other metaphors along the same lines.

Wolfe leaving Pym's got no more than a byline. So there, Wolfe. Yah, boo, sucks.

I spent the rest of the day writing what would be the final report when finished, and making alterations to my speech.

I had intended to go to Pym's late on Wednesday — I needed to see the artwork for the *Daily Mail* to get the grid reference on the supermarket advertisement to get ahead of the traffickers — but received an excited call from Pym. They had had three applications for the post of creative director already, and one was coming in that afternoon. I agreed to meet for a sandwich lunch with him at twelve o'clock prior to the interview an hour later. It was a great excuse for my presence at their offices, so I could sneak around.

Before I left, I spent an hour looking at the accounts of Pym's to see what clever wheezes Norman could come up with for boosting profits and generating cash flow. The more I looked at the investment in Pym's, the more I thought it was money well spent. The diversification of our business seemed like a great idea. As Norman had said, the Shannon brand could be a profitable route to follow.

Pym was bubbling over with excitement. He had spent the morning looking online at the publicity generated by the press conference and taking calls to inquire about roles that might become vacant, not just that of creative director. People wanted to come there.

'You've turned us around!' he said. 'I'm so glad you're on board for the next adventure. I spoke to Sir Gerald this morning, and he said that you should join the board as a non-executive director. Get a first dibs on your time.'

'I would think nothing else,' I said, wondering how I could manage my time out of our core business. I estimated I would now be committed for four days a month, two at Zeus and two at Pym's. 'We need to protect our twenty per cent share. I suggest monthly board meetings, alongside another day for reading the necessary supporting material. With a fair wind, we might be able to move down to bi-monthly. Standard fees would apply.'

Brookie was the best I had seen her since starting work at Pym's. She placed a platter of handmade sandwiches before us with a big smile, and had been able to get an alcohol-free bottle of red wine. Curate's egg.

Nearer to one o'clock, the other members of the board drifted in and finished off what we could not eat. There was elation everywhere, a total reversal in mood since we started work there just about a week or so ago. We should have been popping champagne corks, but best we didn't count our chickens. Or put temptation before Pym.

The candidate was called Sophie, and was tall and slim and dressed in a sophisticated loose jump suit in black. There was a simple chain of gold around her neck and her hair was swept back and secured by two tortoiseshell combs. She had style. Exactly what was needed in a creative director. No Hitler, no zeitgeist, no smoke, no mirrors.

Pym's had a room kitted out as a cinema with a state-of-the-art computerised system capable of handling every format going and a screen the size of Texas. It had ten sofa seats with places on the arms for refreshments. After introductions and handshaking, we filed down the corridor and took our positions, Sophie at the front where she could best answer questions. She took a USB stick and plugged it into the computer. She pressed the button and called up a PowerPoint presentation. The first slide was her name and a running order for what we would hear. The next slide was a CV showing her credentials, job history and current positions. The following slide was the accounts she had worked on. All very professional and impressive.

I could guess why she was looking around: she had hit the glass ceiling where she was and needed a new challenge to show what she could do creatively, given more of a chance. Showed good motivation and a thirst for being stretched.

The slideshow was paused and she took us through a showreel of some of the campaigns she had worked on. The first ad, created as a sixty-second running time for cinema with its younger audience, started with a sweeping vista over the Sahara. The music was dramatic as the camera moved on towards a close-up of the alcoholic drink it was pushing, pouring over ice — you could almost hear the cracking of the ice. It was minimal, it was classy, it was captivating and further emphasised her style as a classy lady. I was blown away.

The commercials progressed through a range of products and services showing her versatility. The room was silent, captivated by her.

It was then back to the slideshow featuring some of the press ads and social media campaigns she had worked on. Showed her flexibility, too.

'I'll now take any questions you have,' she said to a stunned audience.

The questions asked were pretty standard and she batted them away. I kept my awe in check as best as I could.

When it came to the unoriginal question of 'why Pym's?' she had looked across at me with a smile. 'I want to be part of the adventure of where you are going,' she said. 'With the backing of Zeus and Mister Shannon here, this is going to be one of the star opportunities in the industry. And I want it. Badly.'

Pym looked across at me. *Any questions?* he was saying with his raised eyebrow.

'What accounts do you think you can bring with you?' I said.

She mentioned five, including the Sahara drink commercial that had wowed me. Hell, this just got better and better.

'Any creative teams you would want to bring with you?' I asked.

'Two teams who worked on the accounts I mentioned a moment ago.'

'Final question,' I said. 'What is the question we should have asked?'

'They said you were tricksy, Mister Shannon,' she said. 'The usual one is, am I pregnant or planning to be so in the short term? Thanks for not asking. No, I'm not pregnant and don't intend to be so yet. I'm only thirty, and I've got a good few years before I get to that stage. Even then, nowadays with flexible working, it shouldn't cause any disruption.'

'Let me show you out,' I said.

She said her thanks for our time and how good it was to meet us. Shaking hands, she was ready to leave.

I walked her along the corridor to reception. 'Impressive,' I said. 'Hand on heart, can you cut this?'

'I'm hungry,' she said. 'Ready for this. Yes, I believe I can handle this. If it doesn't work, it won't be for want of trying. Trust me.'

'We'll be in touch,' I said.

With a kiss on each cheek, she was locked into the waiting lift. I hoped there'd be more journeys in the wretched machine.

I walked back to the cinema and took my seat again.

'Can you imagine her in new business pitches?' Paul Adams, the account director, said. 'They'd be lapping her up.'

'And that Sahara cinema commercial,' said media director Des Hawkins. 'I could almost feel the sand around my toes.'

'And what's your verdict?' Pym said to me.

'Run up the street after her,' I said.

* * *

I went back to the office allocated in Pym's and worked on the report to deliver on Friday as promised. Not only did it advance the delivery of the report, but it helped to use up time before I thought Tony and Ned would have finished the supermarket advert and gone home.

At six o'clock, I went to the production department, where people were working, as per their contract, on sending finalised ads to newspapers, magazines and so on. I found one of the people and said that I wanted to know more about the department and how it was run.

'Show me a typical ad,' I asked. 'What's involved in the process?'

'This one,' he said, calling the ad up on screen, 'is for fragrance. That's all about image. You can see how the very best is done. The roughs are given to us by the art director. We then produce a final copy with all the bells and whistles. It's easy when you know how and the art director sticks to the rules — doesn't run over time, basically.'

'What about a simpler one that's not all about image, say, the weekly supermarket one?'

He called up the ad on the screen. 'This is the final version,' he said. 'It's tricky because there is a different voucher code for each newspaper. Producing multiple copies, in essence.'

'Can I see the one for the *Daily Mail*? Maybe let me have a copy of this week's one for inclusion in my report?'

'No problem,' he said. He clicked on the screen and then another. He walked over to the laser printer and waited for the page to come out. 'Here you go.'

'So what time would this be able to be read by an actual buyer?' I asked.

'Presses will be ready to roll about eleven. Finished copies printed about midnight and sent to distributors. In shops around four. Swift turnaround, eh? That's the benefit of newspapers, Des would say. Immediacy.'

'Thanks. Much appreciated,' I said.

'Any time,' he said.

Like taking candy from a baby!

The moment I got down to the office, I phoned Palmer.

'I've got the grid reference,' I said.

'Read it over and we'll get the location.'

I read over the six-digit code.

'I'll call you back,' he said.

It only took ten minutes before my phone played out the ringtone of 'Ain't Misbehaving' by Fats Waller, especially for Palmer.

'It's a closed-down caravan site about five miles outside Clacton,' Palmer said. 'Anything else you can tell me?'

'Papers not available to buy until about four or five in the morning,' I said.

'Can't miss the chance of being late. Do you still want to come with me?'

'I'd like to see this strand to the end.'

'I'm only doing this because, without you, we wouldn't have the opportunity. Don't mess up. I'll pick you up at midnight. Bring sandwiches. White bread with crusts taken off and cut into four equal triangles.'

'Butter or spread?'

'Butter,' he said. 'Let's live dangerously.'

CHAPTER TWENTY-ONE

I dressed all in black — jeans, T-shirt, leather jacket and ankle boots — and had a large cool box of assorted sandwiches that Beryl had lovingly prepared to Palmer's instructions. To this she had added a variety of non-alcoholic and energy drinks. There was a flask of coffee, too. She'd also included napkins in the box. She didn't include a picnic blanket.

'What's the plan?' I asked Palmer as we set off.

'We've had a helicopter over the place,' he said. 'There's lots of room for hiding behind derelict caravans. That's where most of the police cars will be hiding — we have two paddy wagons to lock away the perpetrators. We've got others patrolling the streets around the target, watching for trucks entering the area. There'll be others ready to get the coach, too. With one metaphoric blow on the whistle, we shut down the area. We've got police dogs, too, if anyone tries to make a run for it. We've covered all the angles. All we need is for the drop-off to be today rather than tomorrow. We've got your big reveal on Bradley's murder. I have to be there for that.'

'You've got the white lab coat and the plastic gloves ready?'

'As you requested,' he said. 'Will it work?'

'It better have,' I said. 'I've got no other cards to play. You can take away the creative team first — boy, am I looking forward to that — and then assemble everybody I've interviewed. Like you tonight, I think I've covered all the angles.'

'You really care what happens at Pym's, don't you?'

'Even more so now we at Shannon Investigations are twenty per cent shareholders and I'm on the board of directors.'

'You don't waste time, do you?' he said.

'Neither of that was an original direction. I've got to know them after the last couple of weeks. They made one wrong decision and didn't correct it in time. Result — sliding profits and hit on their reputation. I think I can get them back on track. By and large, they're a nice bunch. Financially, they're a bit amateur. There's things that Norman and I can do to make them instantly more profitable — accounting wizardry. And you should have seen the woman we interviewed today for creative director. Wonderful. What a difference she would make. It's all good news. Apart, of course, from Bradley's murder, but we can wash any negative reports with the high point of helping to catch the people traffickers. There's going to be so much positive news around Pym's that no one can ignore. We will become a force in the market.'

We were approaching our destination.

'Let's take a turn around Clacton before we go to the target,' Palmer said. 'Get our bearings.'

'I hope that wasn't a pun,' I said. 'Grid references and bearings.'

'I'm not that desperate,' he said.

Clacton, as we saw from our brief tour, provided much that an average family could want for their holiday. There were fine sandy beaches, arcades for when the weather wasn't good enough to see the sun and a few restaurants and burger vans for the hungry. Even the pier had some wild rides to entice the visitor. It had seen the bad days of lockdown and yet survived. Well, most of it.

We circled back en route, going first on the minor road from Clacton and then on a tarmac track that had seen better days. This was a business that didn't make it. There was a sign saying 'Welcome to Clacton' without mentioning that it was a five-mile walk to where the action took place. This would have been the first place to suffer when the trade crashed during the pandemic and recession.

We parked the car behind a deserted mobile home, which gave us total cover from where the lorry would enter the site and got out to walk around and liaise with the other police vehicles. I turned my collar to the cold and damp and listened to the sounds of silence, as the song goes.

Having reassured ourselves that everyone was in place, we returned to the car and hit the sandwiches.

'Good sandwiches,' Palmer said. 'We should do this more often.'

'Are you expecting any guns?' I said. 'I have a history with guns.'

'I wouldn't have thought so,' he said. 'They won't be expecting any danger. Just a routine job for them, I would have thought, but we have firearms offices in case it gets heavy. Sunrise is about half past six. Should be just getting light when they arrive. If they arrive.'

'They would want, ideally, to get the cargo off as soon as possible,' I said. 'My guess is that they will clear Dover around four, immediately stop for the paper and head here. Give them a couple of hours to get here — they won't want to be caught speeding — and, like you, I would expect them around dawn. Going to be a long wait. Want to play I-Spy?'

'Why did I ever agree for you to come along?'

'My magnetic personality,' I said. 'People just get drawn to me. Mostly assassins, unfortunately.'

'I can see why,' he said.

'If we got out of the car, we could play cricketing fizz buzz,' I said. 'Not enough room for the arm signals in here.'

'Let's get this straight. I do not want to play I-Spy, I do not want to play cricketing fizz buzz, whatever that is. I don't want to play pack my bags, charades or any other game you come up with.'

'Fair enough,' I said. 'Just thought I'd mention it. It's going to be a long wait, you know?'

'I suggest we both doze for an hour or so,' he said. 'Vow of silence, OK?'

I closed my eyes and played GOAT. What would be the best Ashes side of all time England would have played? What was the best West Ham side of all time in the FA Cup?

I dozed.

Palmer's communication equipment barked into life. 'Suspect approaching.'

'All units out of vehicles and stand by,' Palmer said. 'Prepare to block the track behind the lorry and reserve units to watch for a coach or bus. Block that in, too. Ambulances, hold your positions.'

We got out of the car and readied ourselves for action.

'You purely observe,' Palmer said to me. 'You will not get involved. Is that clear?'

'As crystal,' I said. 'You won't even know I'm here.'

'Oh, how I wish I could believe that. Don't let me, down, Shannon.'

The lorry came into view was a dull blue with the logo of a frozen-chip company and had a fan on the roof so that the temperature could be maintained. As it hove into view, the flashing lights were activated on the police vehicles.

'Armed police!' one of the officers shouted. 'Stay where you are!'

Maybe they didn't speak English. Maybe they didn't believe anyone would shoot. Maybe they just didn't care. Whatever, two men jumped out of the cab of the lorry and made a run for it.

One of them must have played rugby as a kid. As the officers came out of their hiding places, one of the men ran directly at the nearest police officer and swerved at the last minute, going outside the officer. The man had broken through the cordon and was making for an escape across the surrounding fields. I waited. I had nothing else to do. So why not?

If he could swerve past one police officer, then he could probably swerve past me. If I couldn't beat him from in front, then it would have to be from the rear. I allowed him to pass.

The very moment he passed me, I leapt out of my hiding place behind the mobile home and ran after him. Morning runs with Arthur proved their worth. I would outpace him easily.

I got closer and closer, dived from behind and grabbed him round the waist, pulling him face down to the ground. I grabbed an arm and twisted it behind his back.

'Don't move,' I said, 'or I will break your arm.'

Judging by the expletive, he did speak English after all. He lay there motionless, my captive.

'I think we'll take him from now on, sir,' one of the police officers said. 'It is our job, you know?'

'You were supposed to keep out of it,' Palmer said.

'Good job I didn't,' I said.

'We would have got him eventually,' Palmer said.

'Just saved you a lot of running,' I said. 'I'll expect a commendation, of course. A quiet ceremony will be fine. Maybe a bottle of fizz in celebration.'

'Come on,' Palmer said resignedly. 'Let's see what's in the truck. We have ambulances here, so don't try any more heroics, like doing a tracheotomy.'

We walked to the lorry and stood there while a police officer forced the lock. He swung the doors open to reveal a wall of cardboard boxes. I heard cries from behind the wall. Police officers cleared the boxes to reveal, when the count was made, thirty frightened illegal immigrants. Some were not moving. The smell was awful. It was the smell of death. My stomach churned and I had to turn my back to stop myself from vomiting.

'Well done, everybody,' Palmer said. 'I'll leave you to do the processing. Come on, Shannon. Time to go home.'

'Some people deserve to die,' I said. 'These didn't. They were just innocent human beings trying to get a better life. OK, they were illegal, but it doesn't warrant this. How do you do this job, Palmer?'

'With time, you develop a hard skin,' he said, 'a sort of tortoise shell that helps to protect you. If you don't, you'd be a like a hedgehog crossing the road: you'd roll up like a ball at the first sign of something bad and get destroyed.'

'I have admiration for you, then. I couldn't do it. I hope with all my might that you'll catch the people responsible for this and shut down this traffic of death. If I get to them before you, I won't be responsible for my actions.'

'Don't even think about it,' he said. 'You can't take the law into your own hands. The days of being a vigilante are over. We'll get them. We've got a start now, thanks to you. Sooner or later, the driver and his mate will squeal and we'll follow the trail to the top. We can hope, too, that there might be some Albanians in prison. You know how rough justice is meted out there. Maybe I'll wash my hands then. Let's go home. We've done what we came here for.'

We drove back in silence. The morning traffic was heavy as we joined the rush of commuters headed for London.

'When will you go public on this operation?'

'They'll be a press briefing around nine or ten, and then the details will start immediately online straight after, and be on the radio news at lunchtime. It will have to wait to hit the press until front page tomorrow morning.'

'Too late,' I said.

I took out my phone and called Shapiro at Zeus. 'I've got a scoop,' I said.

* * *

The reporter was waiting for me when Palmer dropped me off. There was a camera man there, too. I started to wonder what I had let myself in for.

'Coffee, please,' I said to Beryl, whom I suspected, from the bags under her eyes, had stayed up the whole night, too. 'Keep them coming.'

The journalist was called Jeffrey and didn't look like your stereotype hack. He was wearing a blue pinstripe suit, white shirt and red tie. He shook my hand and we sat at the desk in my office. The camera man, Eric, continued to stand

and walked around until he was happy with the shots he would take. I tried to ignore him, but it was hard to do, one's natural instincts being to look straight at the lens. Coffee arrived, and with the first sip I felt more like a human being, although that would soon fade back to disgust.

'I'll start with what happened at sunrise,' I said, 'and fill out whatever background you see as relevant. Let's go.'

It took an hour, and I felt unburdened at the end of it. Maybe catharsis had just happened. Maybe epiphany. Who knows?

* * *

I was just trying to get through the memories and dozing off when I heard a shout from below.

'Nick! Nick!' Anji screamed. 'You've gone viral. There's nobody on this planet who won't know who you are. What great PR. I love you. They'll be making Action Man effigies of you.'

I ran down the stairs into the river room where Anji and Valentine were glued to an iPad. There I was on the screen all in black, unshowered, unshaved, hair sticking up from the short lie-down and not as alert as I should have been. My phone rang. It was Palmer.

'Thanks for letting us police help out with your operation,' he said. 'Boy, you've got a lot of redeeming to do tomorrow.'

CHAPTER TWENTY-TWO

There were five of us crammed into the Beamer: Cherry in the front passenger seat and Anji, Valentine and Morag in the back. I stopped off en route at the jewellers and picked up the rings. I let out a huge sigh of relief. Everything in control. Long may it remain so.

Palmer was waiting outside the offices when we arrived and was carrying a large bag. He was accompanied by three uniformed officers, one of them female. Brusque was about the best I could say for him.

We were over the weight limit on the lift, so had to do it in two journeys. We went first, with Palmer and crew next. We met up in reception where Brookie was waiting as arranged.

'All in place?' I said.

She nodded. 'Everyone assembled, as per your instructions.'

'I'd like you to take minutes,' I said.

'Always willing,' she replied.

We went along the corridor to the boardroom where all were waiting — everybody that I had interviewed during the course of the investigation — minus Wolfe and O'Hara, of course. Long gone. Good riddance. Emma with the multi-coloured hair and oversized glasses gave me a smile. One on my side, at least. There was an intake of breath at the sight of the police. The officers didn't take a seat, but arranged themselves in a line in front of the windows, ready to carry out their duty.

There had been no mention of the involvement of Tony and Ned in the trafficking coverage. I guessed they thought they had got away with it. Oh, sweet revenge.

'All hail the conquering hero,' Tony said, as I walked through the door. How to win friends and influence people. 'I will certainly write that jingle for you now. Something from Homer, maybe. Trojan wars. Heroic deeds.'

'No rush,' I said. 'You're going to have a lot of time on your hands for that.'

Ned merely grunted. As always, he was following in Tony's slipstream.

I made the introductions and we took our seats on one side of the long boardroom table, the interviewees opposite us.

Pym smiled at me, too. 'She's coming,' he said. 'Sophie, that is. We are going places at last. What a happy gathering.'

Unfortunately, I was going to rain on his parade.

'Let's get the show started,' I said. 'Time to thin out the party. Tony and Ned — what are we going to do with you?'

I got an innocent smile from Tony.

I don't know,' I said, 'how you were approached for your role in the illegal trafficking, or how much you were paid each week. I hope you didn't sell your soul for a pittance. You must have thought there was no way you would get caught for your part in the trafficking of illegal immigrants. Three hundred thousand per trip. I hope you got a good cut.'

'If you don't mind, I have copy to write,' he said, rising from his seat.

'Sit back down,' Palmer said. 'We're not finished with you yet.'

'Back to the story,' I said. 'I just wished you had seen what I witnessed yesterday morning and smelt the pungency

179

of death of five people out of thirty. You wouldn't think then that what you were doing was just a bit of fun and easy money.'

'Where is this going, Shannon?' Tony said. He was about to enter the bluffing zone.

'You must have thought yourselves so clever with the coupon codes,' I said.

Tony's face fell.

'Boy Scouts were your downfall,' I said. 'Knowledge of six-digit grid references from the days of shorts, woggles and lanyards. There was a lot of luck on our side, I must admit, but as they say "the harder you work, the luckier you get". Detective Chief Inspector Palmer here knows the law a lot better than I do. What are they looking at? Five years? Ten?'

'Let me see,' Palmer said. 'Aiding, abetting, counselling or procuring an offence under Section 4 of the act? It's that soft heart of yours again, Shannon. Never five or ten years. Can be up to life imprisonment. And then there's all the manslaughter offences — accessory before the fact. Even more serious. Yes, catch a judge on an off day and I'd go for the life option.'

'The irony is that you are just collateral damage to those who do the trafficking,' I said. 'They don't give a damn what happens to you. Do the honours, please, chief inspector.'

Palmer said the words of the caution that have to be said exactly for an arrest. The two male officers helped Tony and Ned out of their seats and escorted them to the door.

'Oh,' I said. 'Just before you go. There's this for you. I haven't worked out the music on the jingle yet, but the words go something like this: "Tony and Ned, get them in prison and they'll wish they were dead". Snappy, eh?'

They didn't seem impressed. What did I care? Palmer was the one soft-hearted this time. He didn't put them in handcuffs. Act one over as they left the room.

'Now for Act Two,' I said. 'Poor Bradley. A man in the wrong place at the wrong time. You see, it didn't have to be Bradley.' There were puzzled looks from that side of the table. 'Yes, Bradley had worked out both the credit-note scam and the coupon device, but that wasn't why he was killed. You see, Bradley died to stop the share placement. The killer couldn't let that go ahead, because it would upset the status quo. Loss of a lucrative trade. Everything had to remain how it was.'

I took a sip of water from one of the bottles on the table. Build the tension, Shannon, rachet up the drama.

'How, the killer thought, could the sale of shares go ahead with one such gruesome death? Slit across the stomach and stabbed in the heart. The killer was taking no chances. Just one act would do it. The attacks on me and my colleagues were all due to the people traffickers — stop our investigation before we had a chance to pick up the importance of the coupon code — and had no relation to Bradley's death. His voluble promise to take his son and wife on the ghost train marked him out for death. The killer didn't care who had to die, as long as someone did. Are you with me so far?'

'And, I assume,' said Des Hawkins, 'the killer is one of us?'

'It's a familiar scene where all the suspects are gathered together in one room,' I said, 'and the big reveal solves the mystery death. Been good for decades now. Got to go with the formula. Yes, one of the people sitting around this table is our murderer. But which one?

'Will it be Emma Potter of the multicoloured hair and big glasses that magnify her sparkling eyes? But where's the motive?

'Then we come to Des Hawkins — the sensible one, loved by everyone. The safe hands. The mediator in resolving disagreements. Interesting. The mole in the camp, biding his time? The natural successor to Vernon, uniting the ship and setting a stronger course?

'How about Harry Barker, head of planning? The worst thing you can say about Harry is that he's nerdy. Not a bad trait to have, though, when social media is something that has to be embraced with open arms, and you're trying to keep pace with the opposition.

'Then there's Paul Adams. Frustrated with his current job. His aim is to have his own agency; maybe a couple of years at Pym's to prove himself and he'll be off. Good with clients, I hear. He can smell a great campaign, so I have been told. Dapper in his three-piece suits. Performs well in new business pitches.

'Then there's Fiona McCloud. Finally getting her due after ten years here. Can she cut the mustard in her new role, or has she been promoted above her capacity? She got the job she wanted — why mess things up by killing Bradley? Makes no sense.

'I suppose we have to talk about Vernon. Did he change his mind about the share sale? Was killing Bradley a desperate move to save face and bring the placement to an end? Possible, but a little far-fetched.'

Des looked at his watch. In the analysis of teams, the first person to look at his or her watch is the team player. Maybe his role of sound hands was the right level for him, rather than team leader.

'Patience, Des,' I said. 'We're getting close to the end. You see, the killer made one mistake.'

'They always do,' said Emma Potter. 'The story wouldn't unfold without the mistake. You can't break the formula, or it ceases to be one. Go ahead, I'm enrapt.'

'May I have the exhibits, chief inspector?'

Palmer opened his bag and passed me what I needed to work the magic.

'Here we have two exhibits,' I said, pointing to where they lay on the table. 'One lab coat covered in blood, as context, and one pair of plastic gloves. We might get some DNA of the killer from it. But there's an easier way. What the killer didn't realise is that with the advances in forensics, the glove can be rolled inside out and a fingerprint taken. I think we'll find your prints on it, Brookie.'

There was a gasp from the audience. Pym went as white as the lab coat in the evidence bag. He didn't move a muscle. Sat there like a statue. From a face of calm when she thought she was there purely to take notes, instead the colour drained from Brookie's face. She sat there stiff as a board.

'You can't be right,' Hawkins said. 'Not Brookie. She wouldn't hurt a fly. She's been here years. She's devoted to the agency. Devoted to Pym, too.'

'When the chief inspector and I were talking about murder, we said that there are only two motives for murder — sex and money. I'm a romantic. I like to see it as love and money. Talk us through it, Brookie. When did you start loving Vernon?'

'They were going to take him away,' she said. Tears started to flow. 'Take my Vernon away from me.'

'Who is they?' I said.

'These people here.' She waved a hand across the table. 'I know what they were planning. They were going to buy Vernon's shares and force him out. Retire him. I wouldn't see him again. I couldn't let them get away with that.'

'How long had you loved him?' I said. 'It was love, wasn't it?'

'Oh, yes. It was love,' she said. 'I'd loved him from the very first day I met him. If only he had not loved her, his wife. We could have been so happy together. Maybe I should have killed her instead. Fifteen years I've loved him. I couldn't bear losing him. He was a true gentleman. It was a pleasure to serve him. Vernon was too good to lose to these people. I couldn't let them get away with it. Someone had to die to make sure of stopping their plan.'

'Tell us about the fair?' I said.

'Such an opportunity,' she said. 'All the people there. Five hundred people to hide among. It was like it was meant to be. I'd taken the knife — one of the long kitchen knives I use to carve a joint — and slit an opening in the canvas earlier in the day. I put the lab coat, knife and gloves by the slit. Then it was just a matter of waiting for the right moment. I slipped in while no one was watching and waited for someone. Bradley was perfect. A client. His death would put a stop to everything. I hid in the dark at the back of the ghost train, and when Bradley came by, I plunged the knife in his stomach and sliced across his belly. Twisted it like they show in the crime stories, so that it wouldn't stick, and then took it out and used all my weight to thrust the knife in his heart.'

Pym still hadn't moved. 'I didn't know,' he said. 'If I did, I might have been able to put an end to things before they had a chance to get so far. To have stopped this senseless death.'

'There was such a lot of blood,' Brookie said, locked into the retelling of her story. 'I never thought it would be like that. When it was done, I took off the lab coat and gloves, placed them at the back of the ride and waited for the screams. I knew everybody would be focused on that sound and moved to where the screams were coming from. It was easy to slip out and join the rush of people and hide among them. I knew there would be confusion. It was all so easy.'

'And if Bradley had survived,' I said, 'what would you have done then?'

'A simple question, Shannon,' she said. 'A simple answer. I would have had to kill someone else. Des was my back-up plan. He was the most liked of the directors. His death would have hurt the most. Caused the biggest reaction. I might have been able to poison him.'

Poison being a woman's method of murder. I didn't know how she hadn't given anyone a clue to her real feelings for Pym. Sometimes mad people can be so devious, and she was mad. That was a certainty. That might get her sent to a psychiatric hospital rather than prison. Diminished responsibility being the defence at the trial.

I turned round at Palmer and nodded.

'I'm arresting you for the murder of Matthew Bradley.' He went into his caution.

'Morag,' I said, 'do your stuff. Look after Pym.'

She walked to where Pym was sitting and placed a hand on his shoulder. 'Let's go to your office,' she said. 'I'll make you a cup of tea. I find that a cup of tea can work wonders.'

The others drifted from the room, leaving the five of us to dwell on what had happened.

'You're a lucky bugger,' Palmer said to me.

'Fascinating,' said Anji. 'I never knew that thing about turning the gloves inside out and getting a fingerprint.'

'I'm not surprised,' I said.

'Why's that?' Anji said.

'Because I just made it up.'

CHAPTER TWENTY-THREE

Honeymoon! Honeymoon!

I awoke on Saturday morning from a dream that had bathed me in a cold sweat and in total panic. I hadn't booked a honeymoon! Surely Cherry would be expecting one. What the hell was I to do? What would be available at such short notice. Maybe Lady Luck would shine on me with some cancellation of someone else's trip to a sun-kissed isle. I wrapped myself in my dressing gown and ran down the stairs.

'Why are you up so early?' Beryl said from her desk. 'You shouldn't be up at this hour. You've got a big day ahead of you.'

'But I forgot to do anything about a honeymoon. I have to get it sorted, otherwise Cherry will be mortified. So few tasks I've had to do and I foul up.'

'Don't worry yourself,' she said. 'It's all arranged. It's a present from all of us — you treat us so generously, we wanted to get you something really special. We've cancelled all your appointments for the week, so you don't need to concern yourself about how we are doing here. You're leaving early on Tuesday morning. Where you're going it will be hot. Pack cool clothes and swimwear, plus a pair of stout boots for exploring. You'll get all the details later. Have patience. Now, get yourself back to bed for an hour.'

'You're a marvel, Beryl,' I said. I'm blessed to be working with you all.'

I went back up to the top storey where Cherry was sleeping soundly — the sleep of the just. I snuggled in beside her and thought about how good my life was.

I dozed until the alarm went off. Then it was all action. I showered, shaved and brushed my teeth. My hair was putting up a fight, and I stuck down the strands that were insisting on misbehaving with gel.

I packed the suit carrier from Chang with my new light grey suit, the blue-and-white-striped shirt with the plain white collar, pale blue tie and other clothes to change into. I put my recently polished shoes into one pouch in the inside of the carrier and everything else in the other one. I checked that I had still got the rings. Nothing left to do, I made my way down to the river room. Norman was there drinking a cup of tea, and I made myself a double espresso. I sat down on the sofa facing the Thames and watched the world drift by.

'I'm ready to go when you are,' he said. 'Arthur and Valentine are meeting us there.'

'Not even time for the condemned man to eat a hearty breakfast?' I said.

'With your nerves,' he said, 'you'd spill it all down yourself. Let's hit the road.'

We loaded up the Beamer and I checked I still had the rings. My fear of losing them meant that I would check many more times during the morning.

'Maybe you should give me the rings,' Norman said, decoding my nervous digging around in my pocket.

I fished around in my pocket and took out the two little boxes that contained the rings and passed them to Norman.

'Don't say anything, Shannon,' he said. 'I will not let them out of my sight. Relax. God, I could do with a beer.'

'Make that two,' I said 'The first thing we'll do when we get there is change, and then head for the bar.'

We were still running early. The traffic, shorn of its commuters on a Saturday morning, flowed well. I drove steadily, not wanting to ruin the day by being caught for speeding, and we pulled in the parking area at the back of the building with lots of time to spare. Arthur's van and Valentine's open-top Beetle were parked already. As a foursome now, we filed into the building and went through the reception formalities and up to our rooms.

'Meet you all outside here in twenty minutes,' I said.

I entered the room — The Groom's Room, said a little plaque — and looked around for the second time. The four-poster bed dominated the room, lending an air of calm and welcoming. The walls were tastefully decorated in a muted blue, the wooden panelling gave solidity and a central chandelier was a touch of class. Someone had spent a lot of time planning the décor so that it accentuated the age of the building, but remained clean and modern. I unpacked my suit carrier and lay everything out on the bed.

I walked into the bathroom en suite and cleaned my teeth, again, and gave myself another spray of deodorant and a splash of fragrance. I changed into my shirt and then my suit. I looked in the full-length mirror and was pleased with the overall effect. Every item looked good on its own and, with synergy, made a great ensemble together. The call of a beer sounded loud in my ear. I opened the door and saw my gathered friends standing waiting for me.

Arthur was wearing his only suit in black. He had livened it up with an RAF-blue shirt with buttoned-down collar and a tie in a bright yellow.

Valentine had on a light grey suit with the thinnest of blue stripes that coordinated well with my own. Pink shirt, no tie. He looked immaculate and would surely have many photographs taken of himself with other guests during the afternoon. Babe magnet.

Norman was wearing a blue suit that we only saw him in at client meetings. He looked more in celebratory spirit with a gingham shirt in blue and pink and a striped tie that probably provided forged entry to some gentlemen's' club to which he didn't belong.

There was an hour to go before the half twelve start of proceedings. We stood at the bar counter and ordered four beers. There were a few other people in the room, none of whom I recognised; I guessed that would be the order of the day. We sat at a table by a window and toasted each other.

'End of an era, Shannon,' Arthur said. 'I never thought this would happen. What girl would be able to like your life-style? Constant puzzlement sealing you off from what reality was going on inside you.'

'And,' Norman said, joining into the spirit of it, 'who would want to be normal alongside your adventurous journeys?'

'If we have finished the character assassination,' I said, 'maybe we can just enjoy our beers. There's not much time.'

'Amazing interview with Zeus,' Arthur said. 'You're the talk of the town. Everybody here will be crowding around you wanting more detail, and the obligatory selfie.'

'Obligatory?' I said. 'You've been swatting up on *Readers' Digest* again, Arthur. Can't have been much on the TV lately.'

'Cosy crime,' Arthur said. 'Can't get away from it.'

Palmer walked into the bar, got a handful of peanuts and a beer. With a glass and a drip mat. He came over to us and dragged a chair from one of the other tables.

'Is this the luckiest man in the world?' he said. 'Marrying the most beautiful woman in the world. He's got a sort of Midas touch, too, but in his case, everything he touches drags up a corpse.'

There was an interruption while Carly, our organiser, asked who we were and then put flowers in our buttonholes — a red rose for me and pink carnations for the others.

'As I said,' Palmer continued, 'he pulled off a real trick yesterday with the plastic gloves. What would you have done, Nick, if she hadn't confessed?'

'Once the secret of her love for Pym was out, there was no point of hiding the rest,' I said.

Campion came into the bar, grabbed a beer and dragged up another chair to our table. 'So my younger friends tell me you went viral — whatever that is. Seems you've hit hero status. All good stuff for Zeus. Great PR. Let's talk more later. Right now, I must take my position, and you reprobates need to get outside. Everybody is taking their seats. Good luck, Nick. You've even magicked up some decent weather. See you at the altar.'

We drank the last of our beers and stood up.

A roll of red carpet had been laid leading up to a small white canopy over a table. Behind the table stood the officiant. Beside him was a smaller table on which there was a collection of books and papers.

We walked up the carpet, me in the middle, Arthur on my left flank and Norman on my right. The seats were now filled with eager watchers, our friends and colleagues in the second row on the left, the first two being reserved for Arthur and Norman. *The Arrival of the Queen of Sheba* was playing through a music system that fed the tune to all the guests. Any time now and it would be *The Wedding March*. I took a moment to take in the surroundings. Behind me was the majestic ancient house, in front of me was the woods, thick and lush with their spring leaves in yellows and greens. The sun was shining and was giving us enough warmth to counteract the soft breeze blowing from my left to where Cherry would stand.

Having no father, Cherry had decided that Sir Gerald would give her away. The music changed. I turned around and saw a vision in white coming up the aisle with Sir Gerald on her right, Cherry with her hand on his arm. The dress was strapless, showing off her coffee-and-cream colouring and accentuating her breasts. The breeze lifted the material of the dress — silk? — and it fluttered around her. Her hair was pinned up and she wore a simple tiara of ox-eye daisies.

Behind her, lifting up the train of the dress, was Anji. She was wearing a long dress in blue and would never be beaten for sophistication. Today she was not the biker girl but a princess.

Cherry was beside me now. We looked at each other and smiled. 'You look marvellous, Walker,' I said.

'You scrub up well, too, Shannon,' she said.

The officiant coughed to get our attention. A hush fell from the audience.

'Dearly beloved,' he said.

And then the service became a blur. I could think of nothing but Cherry.

The officiant bade the audience welcome. Then there was something he said about the joys and responsibilities of marriage and, finally, the exchange of vows.

'I, Nicholas Shannon, take you, Cherry Walker, to be my wife, to have and to hold from this day forward, for better, for worse, for richer, for poorer, in sickness and in health, to love and to cherish, till death us do part, according to God's holy law. In the presence of God, I make this vow.'

Now the same for Cherry.

Except she couldn't speak. She slumped against me, an arrow buried deep inside her. Blood spilling down that wonderful dress.

I heard Arthur shout, 'I'll get him!' and from the corner of my eye saw him running toward the woods. I cradled Cherry in my arms, but she was too weak to stand. I laid her down on the ground, took off my jacket and draped it over her the best I could, tucking it round the arrow so as not to dig it deeper.

Palmer took control of the scene. 'Ambulance is on its way,' he said to me. 'It's going to be all right.'

I took my jacket off Cherry's body and showed him the damage. He winced. There was so much blood.

'They'll start giving her blood in the ambulance,' he said.

I noticed he didn't say *it's going to be all right* this time.

Arthur ran back to where Palmer stood. 'White Audi, reg number . . .' and Palmer read the description through to the person on the other end.

'There's a crossbow dumped in the woods,' Arthur said. 'Foul machine.'

He came over to me and bent down to put an arm around my shoulder. Behind me, I could hear Anji sobbing.

Valentine sprinted over to her and hugged her tight to try to stop the shaking of her body.

The officiant stood like a statue, not able to take in what was happening.

Palmer came over to me.

'Arthur was able to give me the details of the car,' he said. 'Boy, can he move.'

'Why a crossbow?' I asked.

'Silent,' he said. 'Gives more time to get away. He was probably long gone before you realised what had happened. Infernal weapon. Digs deep inside the body. Some of the arrows have barbs on them, so you can't pull them out.'

'It was meant for me,' I said. 'The shooter didn't allow for the breeze blowing left to right. A demonstration of what will happen if you mess with the big boys.'

'We'll catch him,' Palmer said. 'Every police officer in the county will be looking out for him after Arthur's description of the car.'

I heard the wail of an ambulance in the distance and knelt there uselessly, wanting to do everything, wanting to do anything to save her.

Finally, the ambulance arrived and a man and a woman got out and ran to us. They took away my jacket and recoiled — the first time they would have been called to someone who had been shot by a crossbow. They ran back to the ambulance and got a stretcher and moved Cherry on it.

I'm coming with you,' I said.

'Against the rules,' the man said.

Palmer walked over and showed his warrant card. 'He's police,' he said. 'It's his wedding day. Didn't think he would need his warrant card. Let him pass.'

I climbed into the ambulance once they had got Cherry inside, followed by the ambulance woman. The ambulance pulled away and, while moving, a bag of blood was hoisted above Cherry and inserted in her arm. I didn't see how one bag could make good the blood that was pouring out of her.

It took us only fifteen minutes to get to hospital, but seemed a lifetime. Cherry was wheeled straight through to A & E, where she was assessed by a young doctor. 'I need a theatre now!' he shouted.

In a couple of minutes, Cherry was wheeled out, with the doctor going alongside her and me closely following.

'You can't come any further,' the doctor said. 'There's a room for families. You can wait there for her to come out of theatre.'

The room had a small table and four chairs — the most that could be fitted inside. It was meant for breaking the bad news to families, but was too sterile for its purpose. A rack of leaflets provided the only colour. Two of the leaflets were about bereavement. I sat in one of the chairs and let my head fall to my knees. A million thoughts were in my head, none of them good. I took out my phone and called Palmer.

'How's Cherry?' he said.

'She's having an operation now,' I said. 'Take the arrow out and see what the damage is. I don't expect to hear any more for hours. What's happening your end?'

'We got him,' he said. 'We sent along two armed-response teams, but the perpetrator didn't put up a fight when he realised he was cornered. Probably banking on some hotshot lawyer getting him off on a technicality.'

'What happens to him now?' I asked.

'A couple of nights in a cell, and then a routine appearance before the magistrates send him up to the county court. In at nine o'clock and out at five past.'

'Whereabouts is the magistrates' court?'

'It will be City of London. Up near Bank tube station. Don't go getting any ideas. The age of the vigilante is well past.'

'I just want to look him in the eye,' I said. 'I just want to imprint his face in my mind. I've got some serious hate to build up.'

'Valentine drove your car home,' Palmer said. 'So you won't have to go to that place ever again. It will be a long process from here on in. We're looking months before judgment and sentencing. Maybe be more if his lawyers play tricksy and launch appeals. We'll make sure he stays in custody all that time.'

'Is he the top of the chain?' I said.

'I don't think so,' he said. 'The use of a crossbow suggests professional assassin. Who else would use such a weapon? We've got the two men from the illegals' lorry and we'll keep putting pressure on them. One of them, at least, will crack and then we can work our way upstream. We'll get them in the end.'

'And how many innocent people have to die before then?'

'We do what we can,' he said. 'That's all and no more.'

'Keep me posted, Palmer.'

'Will do.'

I cut the call and despaired.

A nurse came into the room. 'It's going to be another three hours or so,' she said. 'If you have something else to do.'

I did.

I got a taxi home.

* * *

I brushed aside anything that anyone would say to me. Got myself a jacket that wasn't covered in blood. Took a wad of cash from the safe and set off in the Beamer.

I parked the car in the usual spot and walked to the youth club. No one there had heard what had happened. I found Buzz playing table tennis and called him outside. I passed him a note.

'This is what I want,' I said. 'I imagine you would know where to find someone who could provide me with what I need.'

He looked puzzled.

'Are you sure about this?' he said. 'This is heavy stuff.'

'Quite sure,' I said. 'I don't have much time. Understand?'

194

He set off and came back twenty minutes later.

'A grand,' he said. 'I think he knows you must be desperate. Still want to go ahead?'

'Never been surer.'

'Follow me.'

Buzz led me past blocks of flats identical to the ones he lived in. There was a pavement café, and he told me to sit. A waitress came by and I ordered a coffee.

A youth in a hoodie showed up and sat opposite me. He waved the waitress away.

'Have you got what I want?' I said.

'Even better,' he said. 'Browning Hi-Power. 9 mm. Packs a hell of a punch.'

'And the bullets?'

'Exactly seven, like you asked. Pass the cash under the table.'

I did as he said. 'Pass the gun.'

He did so. The die was cast.

CHAPTER TWENTY-FOUR

I got back to the hospital just as Cherry came out of theatre. There was a hell of a lot of tubes going in and out of her, and machines with flashing lights and bleeping.

A doctor in scrubs came up to me. 'We've done the best we can,' he said. 'We managed to get the arrow out, but it penetrated a lung. She's functioning on just one lung at the moment. To be honest with you, we don't know if one will be enough. We're taking her to the Intensive Care Unit, where we can monitor her closely. If she has any near family, you might want to get them here. We saved the arrow, in case it was needed by the police for any purposes. If they don't want it, it's yours. That's about all I can tell you.'

Doesn't look good, was the import of his words. I followed him down to the ICU and sat by her bedside.

'We've put her into a coma,' said a doctor on the ward. 'She should heal faster that way. I doubt there's anything else we can do, apart from that. It will be at least twenty-four hours before she comes round. Take faith that we will be watching her, waiting to respond.'

Take faith. I knew what he meant by that. Nothing left to do but pray.

* * *

I spent every waking hour by Cherry's bedside. Sometimes alone, sometimes others came in to check on me as much as Cherry. Beryl brought sandwiches with her and Norman a hip flask of vodka, which I drank greedily and handed back to him for refilling.

Arthur came in. He stood by the bedside, looking down at me. 'Buzz said he's worried about you,' he said. 'He won't tell me why. Says it's a secret between you and him. Anything I should know?'

'Best you don't,' I said.

'How are you getting on?' he said.

'Existing,' I said. 'I'm not important. I have something to do tomorrow morning. Will you fill in for me here?'

'Gladly,' he said. 'Should I ask what you have to do that's so important?'

'Like I said earlier. Best not to know.'

* * *

There was a small crowd at the magistrates' court. No more than a dozen people who had turned up in gruesome fashion, like they used to do in olden days for a hanging. I hoped it would be worth their effort.

I suppose I could have done it when the assassin went into court, but the street by Bank station had too many people going to their workplaces. Best to wait.

When he came out, he was flanked by two police officers. I hoped they'd keep out of it.

A lot of hope going on.

I had seven bullets, that's all, but enough to make a statement. Each bullet had its own purpose.

I took out the gun and fired the first shot into his left kneecap. He slumped down, and the police stepped back from the threat of the gun.

I next shot him in the right kneecap. Then the left hip. Then the right hip. Three bullets left. The next tore into his left wrist. The next into his right.

One bullet left. I pressed the barrel against his head, between his eyes, and began to pull the trigger.

I heard a voice.

'Mister Shannon! Mister Shannon!' Buzz shouted. 'Leave him! There's no honour in killing him. You said never to shoot an unarmed man or a man who is down. He can't harm anyone anymore. Let it go.'

I pressed the trigger and fired the final bullet — into the ground at the side of his head. I dropped the gun and put up my hands in surrender. Buzz hugged me while the police put handcuffs on me.

The rest is left to fate.

* * *

Palmer found me in the cells at the police station. 'You've done it this time, Shannon. What possessed you?'

'The medium is the message,' I said. 'The medium was the gun. The message was, you can't get away with harming my wife and my friends. Do so and you will pay for it.'

'Have you got a good lawyer?' Palmer said. 'Because you're going to need one. Assault with a deadly weapon. Possession of a firearm. GBH. All in the morning light where everyone could see your face. Your lawyer is going to earn his keep. Use your one phone call.'

'I already have. He'll be here soon.'

'I know what you're going to ask, and I don't know how I can do it. Doesn't seem much chance of seeing Cherry.'

'If she dies, I see no point in living. If she lives, there are friends who will look after her. Ironic, isn't it? The story began in prison years ago, and will end with me back in prison.'

'At least you didn't kill him,' Palmer said.

* * *

'At least you didn't kill him,' said Martin, my lawyer.

We were sat in an interview room, opposite each other. The table between us was bolted to the floor. The top was covered in rings where too many cups of hot tea had been placed over the years. The walls were stained from nicotine, from those days when you could smoke. Chain smoke, probably. The chairs were wood and started a pain in your back after the first five minutes of sitting down. A uniformed officer stood at attention at the door with a frown on his face.

'Let's review the situation,' Martin said. 'Point one. You will plead guilty to all the charges — no point denying anything. Point two. I imagine you would like to go to the hospital to see Cherry. Are we agreed so far?'

'Agreed.'

'Point three,' he said. 'You have been working with the police. Got to count for something. The best I can do is try to get you two years, then I can look at a suspended sentence. Your crimes carry a much longer tariff. I'm going to have to come up with something special. There is one good point. You seem to have a habit of going viral. Someone took a video of what happened. It's all over the internet, every social media site. There's some negative feedback, of course, about taking the law into your own hands, but the vast majority of the public are with you. They believe that you should walk free. There's a groundswell building up. We might just be able to take advantage of that. First things first. Let's talk to Palmer.'

The officer on the door relayed a message, and Palmer came back in. He shook Martin's hand. Good sign.

'I've got a proposition to put to you,' Martin said. 'I assume Nick will have the customary appearance in front of the magistrates' court.'

'Correct,' said Palmer.

'Are you happy with him not attending in person? He'll be passed on to the county court anyway — with the backlog in cases, it could be a year before that happens. I will plead for some compassionate treatment in regard to Cherry,' said Martin. 'I want him to be able to go to the hospital to see her. If he hands over his passport and agrees to have a tracker fitted, will you object?'

'It might look heavy-handed if I did, especially considering the tidal wave of sympathy that's going on. I would have no objection to those conditions.'

'Agreed,' said Martin. 'Now let's look a further time ahead. Nick will presumably be taken into police custody. Him having showed compassion to the assassin, would you oppose bail — tracker fitted, daily reports to a police station, anything else you want to have?'

'I don't see that he would be any threat to the public,' said Palmer. 'The opposite, it would seem. Might be a PR coup for the force.'

'Would you be agreeable to take statements at the hospital rather than here?' Martin said.

'No objection,' said Palmer.

'Then let's get him out of here,' Martin said.

* * *

Valentine was sitting by Cherry's bedside when I got to the ICU with a female police officer by my side. He gave me a hug, and there was a tear in his eye.

'So good to see you,' he said. 'I know I'm only the junior member of the team, but I feel as much for Cherry as any of us. We've all been so worried about you. How are you able to come here?'

'I've got a very good lawyer, and Palmer has pulled out all of the stops. Any update?'

'A doctor did his rounds at nine o'clock. He didn't say much, so that might be good news. Cherry is breathing better, and is due to come out of the induced coma about now. The picture will look clearer when that happens, he said.'

Valentine got up from the chair and we swapped places.

'I've got some fantastic news,' he said. 'The video of your attack on the assassin has gone viral. I suppose you knew that. What you don't know is that Buzz is a national hero. His speech about honour has fired up everyone's imagination. There's money pouring in from everywhere to what is being called Buzz's Place. Norman and I have opened an account for it and started to set up as a registered charity, with him and me as trustees. So far, the total is three million pounds.'

'Three million?' I said. 'Are you sure? You've not made a mistake, have you?'

'Have you ever known Norman to make a mistake over money? I've done some digging on the second-hand furniture store next door and the landlord has agreed to us taking over the lease. We won't need much for that, and our plan is to roll out the format to other areas. It won't be long before there will be Buzz's Places springing up all over the country. So, don't despair. Something good has come out of your actions. I'll leave you now. I expect everyone will want to come in and see you and Cherry. If there's anything you need, give us a call.'

I reached over from the chair to take hold of Cherry's hand. It was icy cold. I wanted my warmth to spread to her, just like I wished I had taken the arrow instead of her.

'Get yourself a chair,' I said to the police officer. 'You can't stand up all day. Let's get this statement done.'

It took two hours to do. The woman police officer — Jane — wasn't a fast writer, and there was a lot to include. Jane got us coffees twice and we got to know each other — she had two young boys that she was managing to bring up as a single parent while holding down a full-time job. *Kids*, she had said. *Who'd have 'em?*

All that time, I held Cherry's hand. And then it happened. I felt a flutter. Her fingers had moved. Then she opened one eye.

'Good to see you, Shannon,' she said quietly, with a rasp due to not operating fully on both lungs.

'Good to see you, too, Walker,' I said. 'You had me worried for a while.'

'Are we married?' she said.

'I rather hope we aren't,' I said. 'That way we can do it properly another time.'

'I have something to tell you,' she said.

'Fire away.'

'I'm pregnant.'

Gulp.

'Twins.'

Gulp. Gulp.

'Such wonderful news,' I said. 'You know what that means.'

'Which is?'

'I've had a Damascene moment. Epiphany. Rebirth. Whatever you like to call it. Things are going to be different from now on. At the first sign of danger, we quit.'

And that was the promise I made. Time would tell.

THE END

THE JOFFE BOOKS STORY

We began in 2014 when Jasper agreed to publish his mum's much-rejected romance novel and it became a bestseller.

Since then we've grown into the largest independent publisher in the UK. We're extremely proud to publish some of the very best writers in the world, including Joy Ellis, Faith Martin, Caro Ramsay, Helen Forrester, Simon Brett and Robert Goddard. Everyone at Joffe Books loves reading and we never forget that it all begins with the magic of an author telling a story.

We are proud to publish talented first-time authors, as well as established writers whose books we love introducing to a new generation of readers.

We have been shortlisted for Independent Publisher of the Year at the British Book Awards three times, in 2020, 2021 and 2022, and for the Diversity and Inclusivity Award at the Independent Publishing Awards in 2022.

We built this company with your help, and we love to hear from you, so please email us about absolutely anything bookish at feedback@joffebooks.com

If you want to receive free books every Friday and hear about all our new releases, join our mailing list: www.joffebooks.com/contact

And when you tell your friends about us, just remember: it's pronounced Joffe as in coffee or toffee!

ALSO BY PAUL BENNETT

NICK SHANNON THRILLERS
Book 1: DUE DILIGENCE
Book 2: COLLATERAL DAMAGE
Book 3: FALSE PROFITS
Book 4: THE MONEY RACE
Book 5: BLUE ON BLUE
Book 6: SHANNON'S LAW
Book 7: SHANNON'S GAMBLE
Book 8: SHANNON'S REBIRTH

JOHNNY SILVER THRILLERS
Book 1: MERCENARY
Book 2: KILLER IN BLACK
Book 3: ONE BULLET TOO MANY
Book 4: NO EASY WAY OUT

STANDALONE NOVELS
CATALYST

www.ingramcontent.com/pod-product-compliance
Lightning Source LLC
Chambersburg PA
CBHW020618180626
46810CB00007B/2830